AF241688

Abracadabra
I love you

John Nieman

Contents

Dedication

For Mary Ellen

Chapter 1

arc Obie sat in the fifth seat of row three at Hastings Grade School. As usual, he had several distractions.

Primary among them was Pat Foley, the most beautiful young girl in the school who sat right across the row from him. Like every young boy in class, he had noticed her for the last several weeks. A cute brainiac, she paid attention to the teacher and often raised her hand with the right answer.

By contrast, Marc was a less than average student. Just to make matters worse, he was not a basketball player, or a standout at dodgeball.

As the teacher, Margaret Carlson, finished her arithmetic puzzle on the blackboard, he looked around at the class. "I have written 7 and 5, with a line underneath. What's the total? " Of course, Pat Foley had her arm waving in the air, but as Ms. Carlson already knew, that was just too easy. She needed to involve less interested members of the class. "Anyone? Anyone?"

She then looked at Marc, who was playing with strings on his desk. "Marc Obie, what's the answer?"

"I'm sorry," Marc answered. "What's the question?"

"What is seven plus five?"

"More than 10," Marc answered, and the class laughed. He looked across at Pat Foley who still had her anxious hand waving in the air, and did steal a look at the curious paper threads on his desk.

After a few guesses of "more than eight, and more than nine." He finally conceded, "I don't know."

Mrs. Carlson did exude a frustrated sigh. After all, even in the first grade, a kid should be able to count this high. "Use your fingers, Marc. Count up to seven and then five."

After a few minutes, the kid shook his head no. "I don't have that many fingers. I only have ten." There were a few giggles in class. Rather than demonstrate the obvious, the teacher stared at the floor. She then looked back and the class of eager answerers with their hands in the air.

"Miss Foley," the teacher said. "You've had your hand in the air for some time. Do you know the answer of seven plus five?"

"Seven plus five equals 12," the young girl proudly proclaimed.

"That's correct," the teacher said.

As soon as she did so, Pat looked across the aisle with a big grin on her face. She looked at Marc, but he didn't respond to her braggadocio. Instead, he seemed to completely preoccupied with two strings, which he was fingering carefully.

Eventually, the math lesson was over and the bell rang for recess. All the kids immediately rose from their desks and exited for a little fresh air. Most of them ran straight to the playground just to escape the addition and subtraction preliminary lesson.

When Marc hit the outside, he took a deep breath and enjoyed the outdoors. Soon, he was joined by the little, lovely Pat Foley. "I saw those strings on your desk,," she said. "What were you doing?"

"Just a surprising miracle," he shrugged.

"Show me," she reacted with a smile.

Marc reached in his pocket and took out the strings. They were tied at both ends. "Point to one," he requested.

She pointed to the one on the left. "Pick it up," Marc replied. "I'll take the other end." Then he invited her to untie the knot, while Marc seemed to do the same on his end.

Suddenly, Marc proudly smiled, anticipating a response. He separated the two strands in Pat's hands and held the other bundle in his right hand. He then asked her to spread her two strings apart. As she did so, he opened his hand to show that—lo and --there was no longer a knot in his hand. In fact, there were no longer two strings-- just one string, with one end in Pat Foley's left hand and the other in her right hand.

The little girl screamed with joy. "How did you do that?" She rubbed her hand on the one string and could see nothing unusual about it. "Wow, that's great," she laughed. "How did you do that?" she repeated.

"It's magic," Marc proudly answered.

"You should have shown that to Mrs. Carlson," Pat advised. "She wouldn't have been so hard on you."

"Aw, she wouldn't understand." Marc wisely smiled. As a very young budding magician, he had already learned that people had to be in the mood for miracles. If not, they would simply criticize him as a loony.

"How did you do that?" Pat innocently asked.

"I can't tell you. It's a secret," Marc proudly said. He instinctively knew that she was a young, but appreciative audience.

The two began to walk to the swings and the see-saw. Before they could reach the actual playground, the bell rang, signaling a time to come back to class.

"Will you show me another trick some day," Pat Foley honestly asked with an admiring smile.

"I promise," Marc answered and proudly entered the classroom for the next academic lesson in spelling. Unlike the morning class, he decided to give this teacher some responsiveness. Buoyed by his new budding relationship, he decided that some attention to spelling f-r-i-e-n-d might be a very good thing.

Chapter 2

By the time Christmas rolled around, the classroom (in fact, the entire Catholic school) was decorated with trees, wreaths, and lots of colorful lights.

Not surprisingly, it was difficult to keep the kids' attention on reading, writing and arithmetic when they are obsessed with creating lists of possible presents and winter vacations.

Pat Foley and Marc Obie remained friends, but at that age, it was extremely casual relationship. True, she had some admiration for the boy's unexpected magic, and he had some true attraction for her interest in his sleight-of-hand. As he had requested, it was their little secret, and it created an unusual, unrevealed bond between the two of them.

Marc had learned these pocket tricks from his uncle Ray, who was a working magician. Ray had a regular gig at a nightclub and occasional appearances at various gatherings. Whenever he would get together with his nephew, uncle Ray would try to share some marvelous miracles. Marc was always a mesmerized audience and often pleaded with uncle to teach him a few tricks.

Knowing that most of his effects were beyond the ken of a 7-year old, Uncle Ray did share a few easy mysteries. No card handling. No difficult moves. Most of what he shared with young Marc were what trained magicians call "gimmicks"-- self-working apparatuses that are hand-held and can still create amazement to an unsuspecting audience.

Ray urged his young protégé to work hard on the tricks and not reveal the secret of the effect. He asked one other promise. "When people ask you how you did that, you must not reveal the true answer. Just say, 'it's magic,'"

"I already did that when I showed a friend the string that magically is restored," young Marc retorted with a puffed up chest of accomplishment.

"So great! You've already learned the No. 1 secret to being a magician," Uncle Ray beamed. He then went on to teach his willing pupil a few, new easy-to-perform amazements.

One particular example was the thumb tip, which came in handy for Marc at his Christmas celebration at school.

He was standing next to Pat Foley at the time when the principal had gathered everyone in the cafeteria for the lighting of the Christmas tree. All the kiddoes were singing Christmas carols when the principal finally asked for some quiet from the assembly.

He then pointed to the tree and asked the students to count down. 10-9-8-etc. At the count of 1, the lights were turned on and the kids all got in line for some fruit juice and a brownie.

While everyone was milling around, Marc found Pat Foley and compared notes about their different Christmas plans.

Eventually, Pat told the young boy that she would be travelling to Florida to be with her grandparents during the holidays.

"Do they have Christmas trees down there?" Marc asked.

"Of course," Pat answered.

"With lights?" Marc probed.

"Duh, of course," the young girl answered.

"I love the lights," the budding magician acknowledged. "Especially that red one on the right side of the tree." He looked for a response from Pat, but there was none at the moment. "Watch this!" he teased.

He then reached in his pocket and pointed to that red light he had earlier referenced. With an open hand, he then waved his hand and produced a bright red light on his right thumb.

"Wow, that's terrific." Pat said with wide eyes.

"It's just a red Christmas light," Marc shrugged. He then opened his right hand and flashed a gesture to the tree. At once, the red light on his thumb disappeared. He then pointed to the tree with his right finger. "There! It's back on the tree."

"Yikes. That's amazing!" young Pat screamed. "Do that again for my friends!" Then the young girl motioned for her girl friends to join her.

"No, that's just for you," Marc responded.

When her friends had joined her, Pat was good enough to not reveal the trick or ask for a repeat. "Let's wish each other a Merry, Merry Christmas," she said. Within a few second all of them raised their juice cups and saluted the moment.

Marc and Pat stole a private look at each other. At the time, Marc gave her a high-five…partly for the sentiment of the moment, and partly for her desire to keep their magic a secret.

Chapter 3

It's only natural that middle-schoolers separate by gender. Girls begin to discover fashion and flirting. Boys begin to learn macho sports and naughty jokes.

Such was the case of Pat Foley and Marc Obie.

Pat, as could be predicted from her early academic success, had that same devotion to success in her appearance. She had that kind of flair that is actually rare at this age. She also tended to love those creative accessories that make a young woman more attractive—scarves, hats and caps, and of course, shorter skirts. Don't worry, she didn't turn into an Instagram moonie. True to her talents, she continued to do well in school and earn good report cards.

She did have an extracurricular escape, and it played into a secret gift of hers—the ability to sing. This was first evident in her choir classes, when at a very young age, the music teacher recognized that she could easily carry a tune, and even capture the emotion of a song. Once her parents heard about this ability of their young daughter, they did encourage it. On a once a week basis, they provided voice lessons for young Pat. Not surprisingly, she became an amazing young star of the music school's annual recitals.

By contrast, Marc strove to find some acceptance with the buddy culture. He enjoyed hanging out with fellow students at the malt shop to talk about NFL teams and the latest movies. By now, a lot of his young friends were playing soccer in a little league (and Marc did occasionally join them purely for social reasons) but his main passion remained magic.

His Uncle Ray loved having a young willing protégé, who had a sincere interest in all his miraculous effects. Ray would demonstrate a trick, mostly to entertain young Marc. However, knowing the lad's interest in sleight-of-hand, the uncle would occasionally share his secret maneuvers. Cognizant of the boy's age and skill level, he would guage his lessons to manipulations that Marc could perform. There was still a minimum of complicated card moves. To help, Uncle Ray gave him a small mirror to observe his technique and a few books of easy-to-learn magic. Predictably, Marc studied them assiduously. Yes, probably more than his academic textbooks from school, but the young boy did work hard enough to do decently in the middle grades.

If he ever hit a snag, he always had a friend called Pat Foley who he could get him out of a jam. For some reason, ever since he showed her a trick or two, (and she had wisely never revealed the secrets), they had a special bond. Despite their normal predisposition for same-sex friendships, both seemed more than willing to make an exception in each other's case. Consequently, at an early age, they had a special relationship.

On one of their school recesses, Pat asked Marc if he was thinking about doing a trick at the middle school talent show.

"I don't know," Marc honestly answered. "When is it?"

"It's in March. Auditions are in about 3 weeks. You should definitely do a trick or two."

"Think so?" Marc proudly beamed at the compliment.

After a few seconds, Pat volunteered a thought. "I am thinking of auditioning, too."

"You do magic?" Marc incredulously asked.

"No, silly. I was thinking of singing a song," she shrugged.

"Wow, that's great. So we could be in it together. Fantastic," he added. Instinctively, Marc knew that his soccer buddies would not have anything to offer in a talent show. But it would be nice to share the experience with a friend. "I'm going to do it. And I am proud of you that you're going to do it too. Good luck to both of us."

They both gave each other a thumbs up, and waved goodbye as they joined their other classmates on the playground and ball field.

Chapter 4

Despite the fact that very few of their friends had auditioned for the middle-school talent show, the school auditorium was filled with spectators and students on the evening of March 18.

Pat Foley's mom and dad had seats in the front row. They still weren't quite sure about their daughter's relatively recent fascination with singing, but thought she was good in their home rehearsals, and had supported her in voice lessons. They were definitely proud of her academic achievements, and wanted to give her every encouragement in all her pursuits.

Marc had practiced a few routines with Uncle Ray and settled on one that both agreed could entertain the audience and showcase his magical talents. Ray, and Marc's mom and dad sat in the fourth row, and had witnessed his private rehearsals many times at home.

The actual show began with the pledge of allegiance from the entire assembly. When it was done, Mrs. Davenport, the drama teacher of the school acted as the m.c. for the evening took the stage and addressed the audience.

"I am so pleased that we have such a large audience on behalf of our young performers. As many of you know, this is not a contest. Everyone did have to audition to get in the show, and attend every one of our eight rehearsals. I am so proud of how much effort each of the students have put into their acts. And I really encourage you to give each of the performers a nice round of applause and your own personal encouragement. It's a good thing that they have the courage to perform in front of you. It's also part of their life-long journey to find the things that make them click. So let's welcome our first performers—a tap-dancing act featuring three of our third-graders—Anna White, Linda Markus, and Ginger Johnson. Let's give them a nice round of applause.

With that, a recorded piece of music began to play. It was "At the Hop" from Danny and the Juniors. The three young students were mostly in a line, but occasionally one would take center stage and do a split or a fancy slide. It was not exactly precision, However, when they would hear the cue to hop, often all three would jump off the ground… which the audience seemed to enjoy.

At the end of their short number, Mrs. Davenport walked to the microphone applauding, and encouraged the audience to do the same.

After that, the drama teacher introduced acts of tumbling. Then two boys brought out bongo drums and basically kept pace with the next recorded beat. Then there was a ballet routine over classical music. All of these participants gained a nice smattering of applause.

After about 35 minutes, Mrs. Davenport asked the audience to quiet down and get prepared for something special. "Boys and Girls, Ladies and Gentlemen…it is now time for a solo singing act. Bear in mind how much guts it takes at this age to come on this stage all alone and sing a song. But we have such a performance tonight. Please welcome Pat Foley who will sing "Somewhere Over the Rainbow."

With that, Pat entered the stage from the left wing and took center stage, while the lights dimmed just a little, and a visual of a bright rainbow illuminated the back curtain. She was dressed in an outfit similar to the one Judy Garland wore in the movie. As the karaoke version of the song began to play, she looked at the rainbow and began to sing.

Marc, watching from the right wing, couldn't help but notice the mesmerizing effect that she had on the audience. For one thing, her voice was sweet as honey. Her gestures were clean and effortless. As the number built to its climax, she pointed again at the rainbow, then at the audience, and then took a bow.

There was thunderous applause. When it began to die down, Pat blew a kiss to the audience and skipped off the stage.

Marc was actually amazed at the performance and the reaction. He had no idea, she had that much talent.

After a few seconds, Mrs. Davenport took center stage again and nodded in agreement with the audience. She then introduced a few more acts. Next was a baton twirler, who got some meager applause. Then a violin player, who made a few goofs, but muddled through the performance. He was followed by three cheerleaders who roused the audience in a positive way.

When Mrs. Davenport, the emcee, took the stage, she introduced the last act. "And to close out our talent show, we have a special treat—a magician who will absolutely amaze you. Watch him closely, and you will wonder how in the world did he do that? Boys and girls, Ladies and Gentlemen, please give a nice round of applause for Marc Obie."

With that, Marc skipped towards the center stage wearing a black suit that his Uncle Ray had bought him just for this occasion. He was carrying a small bag that contained some grocery ingredients. Then he paused and addressed the audience. "I want to show you how to make a delicious treat. So this is sort of a cooking lesson."

The music started to play. It was a song from Oliver called "Food, glorious food."

Marc began his routine by taking out a magic prop called the Dove Pan. It looked like a cooking pot with a lid. He then lifted the top of the lid and showed an empty pot. One by one, he began to put in ingredients.

"For this recipe, you will need some flour." He opened up a jar and poured some of the white powder in the pan.

"You will also need some sugar." He then added this ingredient.

"How about some blueberries? Some milk. Some baking soda." One by one, he added each item. "Oh my gosh. I almost forgot. This recipe needs two eggs."

He then cracked two raw eggs on the corner of the pan and poured them in with the rest of the contents.

Then he paused. "Where is the oven? How am I going to bake this?" he teased.

Almost as if he a stroke of inspiration, he reached in his coat a pulled out a magic wand. "One of the nice things about being a magician is that I can make it happen without a stove. Watch!"

He then put the lid on the pot and touched it three times with his magic wand. "As they say in my Spanish class, "Uno, Dos, Tres… and abracadabra!"

He dramatically lifted the lid of the pan, and told the audience, "I think it's done."

He then reached into the pan and pulled out four perfectly-baked muffins.

"Who likes blueberry muffins?" he asked the audience. Instantly, hands were raised from many members of the audience.

The magician took a few muffins and tossed them in the air. "One muffin for you," he shouted. "And one muffin for you," he repeated. He then threw one muffin to the left and one to the right to loud applause.

"Who else wants a muffin?" he again teased. "One for you in the center. One for you in the back. And that's the way a magician makes blueberry muffins!"

There was a loud and long ovation. Marc waved the audience, took a proud bow and exited the stage.

Mrs. Davenport, the emcee again came to the center of the stage. She herself was clapping. "I'd like to thank all the performers who shared their creativity today." She then introduced them one by one and asked them all to stand in a line. There was a nice applause for each act, but by far, the biggest applause was heard for Pat Foley and Marc Obie.

The emcee then asked the crowd to quiet a bit. "I would like to thank you all for being a good audience, and end the show by asking all he participants in the talent show to take one more bow all together. One. Two. Three."

She then waved to the audience and scurried the group off the stage.

"Good night everybody. Hope you all enjoyed. Have a safe trip home, "Mrs. Davenport called out, and then exited the stage.

Most spectators, parents, and fellow classmates agreed it was a spectacular, memorable evening.

Chapter 5

As soon as the performers left the stage, they spread out into the audience to bask in the kudos and meet up with their friends. There were many slaps on the back, hugs and handshakes.

The praise was varied, depending on the act and the source.

"Congratulations. I was so proud of you."

"Wow, that was just great."

"The whole show was wonderful, but you were especially amazing,"

Pat Foley had heard many of these salutations backstage, but when she crossed into the auditorium, she was deluged with praise. From the corner of her eye, she could see her mom and dad who were high-fiving her and pantomiming applause. After a little chit-chat with her admirers, she did work her way to her parents.

"That was breathtaking," her mom acknowledged and gave Pat a big hug. To her left, her father was beaming. He was also holding out a muffin, which he had caught from Marc's magic performance. "Hungry?" the dad kidded his daughter.

"Where did you get that?" Pat asked her dad.

"I caught it," he giggled. "It was really a nice performance. You and the magician were the stars of the show. And each of you got the most applause."

Pat motioned to her father to be shush up. "As Mrs. Davenport told us all at the first rehearsal, this was not a contest. Eveyone who participated deserves to feel great."

"Maybe so," Dad nodded his head, but then shrugged. "Even so, you and that magic guy really captured the emotions of the audience." As she heard this, she also noticed Marc, who had just come from the stage and had begun to mingle with the audience. As she saw him, she motioned for him to join her with her parents.

Amid some more pats on the back from classmates, Marco did join Pat and her folks. 'Marc, I want to introduce you to my mom and dad. They really liked your performance."

The young magician beamed and extended his hand to shake with Mrs. Foley, and then to Mr. Foley, who was still holding the muffin.

"Wow, where did you get that? Did you bring it from home, or did you catch it?" Marc innocently asked.

"I caught it in mid-air from one of the stars of the show," Mr. Foley said. "You were great," the dad gushed.

"Thanks," Marc answered, and without much hesitation, turned the tables to Pat. "I thought she was spectacular. You were good at rehearsals, but here in front of a big audience…Wow! Did you hear that applause you got, Pat?"

Pat nodded and her dad smiled. "I think I like this guy. He's got class."

As their chit-chat continued, more classmates came to congratulate the two performers. As they did so, Marc saw the waves of his Uncle Ray and his mom and dad a few rows up. "Pat, let me introduce you to my parents and my Uncle Ray. Come with me."

She agreed and excused herself from her parents. When the two reached Mr. and Mrs. Obie and Uncle Ray, there were hugs all around.

"You my dear, have some real talent," Ray said and theatrically kissed her hand.

"And he would know," Marc winked at Pat. "He's a real showbiz guy. A professional magician who taught me everything I know. "

"Didn't I tell you that giving free food to people was quickest route to audience applause?" Ray teased.

"Yep, you did."

Marc's mom decided to turn the subject back to the young lady. "I really enjoyed your song, Pat. It's from one of my favorite musicals, and I thought you were every bit as good as Judy Garland."

"I agree," Dad added.

As Pat was blushing, one of her girl friends joined the crowd and tapped on the shoulders of Pat and Marc.

"We're all going to Lombardo's to get an after-show pizza. There will be a nice crowd there. Lots of classmates…and parents and friends are invited. Come join us!"

Marc motioned to his parents and Uncle Joe with a gesture of "What you think?"

"It's a good idea," Mr. Obie agreed. "Pat, would you like us to give you a ride?"

"Aw thanks, but that's not necessary. My folks are here with me, and they may be hungry, too."

"OK, hope to see you there," Marc answered and gave her a friendly hug.

They all headed to Lombardo's, which had the best pizza in town. There was quite a good crowd. Lots of students. Lots of parents. Even Mrs. Davenport and stage managers came to join the fun. Given the popularity of their acts, Pat and Marc made the rounds between the tables, but still found time to have a slice or two of pepperoni.

For each of the most popular performers, it was a very tasty evening.

Not surprisingly, both secretly wished it would just be an appetizer of more good things to come.

Chapter 6

For most middle-school students, it's a big leap to high school. A big part of that is the fact that high schools are often fed by several middle-schools. That means more students, more activities, more clubs and the potential for a lot more friends.

Such was the case of Hamilton High School, particularly for the two stars of the Hastings middle-school talent show. Yes, they retained some limited contact during the summer—a few days at the pool, and some schoolmate barbecues. However, like most 13-year old kids, there were family vacations and newly-discovered personal pursuits.

For many weeks in July, Pat had the privilege of visiting with her grandparents in Miami. They had given their granddaughter this as a graduation gift for her middle-school graduation. As active, affluent, mid-fifty relatives in a desirable location, it was a dream trip for young miss Foley. They often went sailing on Grandpa's catamaran. They dined on Espanola Way, where Pat could sample new kinds of cuisine and practice her Spanish. They took a weekend trip to Key West, where Pat saw more gay people than she had ever seen, even in New York City. Perhaps the highlight of the trip was a visit to a local Karaoke club, where grandpa and Grandpa demurred, but Pat amazed her grandparents with a beautiful rendition of "What's Love Got to Do with it," the hit made famous by Tina Turner.

By contrast, Marc had no such prosperity in his family. His mom and dad were very hard-working middle class parents, who simply wanted to raise their son with good values. They did have a newfangled cable TV, where he could watch his favorite classic movies. Of course, he also had his Uncle Ray, who was more than happy to school his nephew in new, slightly more advanced tricks. Ray often performed on Monday Night Magic—and despite his young age, Marc was able to occasionally attend, as long as he was accompanied by his father.

By September, both kids were individually exhilarated about all the new challenges of high school. Other than the school bus, which they both took each day, they had very different classes. In fact, the only class they actually shared was social studies. True, they would see each other at high school football games and general assemblies….but it was not the same.

Marc couldn't help but notice that Pat was quite a popular young girl in the freshman class. At lunchtime, she was often surrounded by new classmates. Many of them were new young boys that had come from different middle schools.

As far as Marc could remember, it was his first hint of jealousy. Deep inside, he told himself, that he should do the same thing. Talk to his new classmates, Meet the new guys. Flirt with the new girls. But something in his nature automatically resisted.

Funny thing was, if he had a magic trick in hand, he could be very outgoing. Perhaps that's why he liked those tricks. It had a strange knack for getting him out of his shell.

As the fall passed into winter, both kids settled in their new environment. They would have slightly different paths ahead…but both had a secret admiration for each other, and some faint hope that they would always remain friends, and perhaps even grow closer in the years to come.

Chapter 7

Given his nephew's interest in magic, Uncle Ray thought it would be a good idea to enlist the young kid in the Society of Young Magicians. It was a fairly easy process of signing a pledge to improve the art of magic, not tell any of the secrets of magic to anyone who is not a magician, and strive to use magic in a positive way for personal enjoyment and for the amazement and enjoyment of family, friends and others.

Joining the groups had several advantages. Once in, he was entitled to a membership card, pin, access to the youth newsletter, and M-U-M, the monthly magazine of the grown-up Society of American Magicians. There were other more personal benefits: the development of self-esteem, learning the discipline of practice, and interacting with other kids who had similar interests.

Marc loved belonging to the group. He made several new friends—Bobby, Carlos and Barry—each of whom were about at the same skill level. Once every Saturday at the meetings, they would all got together and practiced new effects. Occasionally, each of them would do a routine in front of the small group. In Marc's first performances, he wowed the group with a few card tricks, and later with one that involved sponge balls.

Mom, Dad, and Uncle Ray appreciated the effect on Marc. He seemed to beam with pride and glow with an inner peace. This self-confidence seemed to even affect his days at school, where he walked the halls with more poise. It even manifested itself in his grades, which had magically improved since middle-school.

His Uncle Ray wanted to keep the ball rolling and invited Marc to be his guest and attend the annual Society of American Magicians convention. It was in Las Vegas this particular year, and attracted more than 1000 practicing magicians. Yeah, it was a big deal, and the event of the year.

In advance, Marc asked his uncle if he would need to perform there. "Oh, no, no," Ray answered with a laugh. "This is a huge national convention, and we are the guests. We'll see some big shows on the main stage, but there are also lots of other attractions. There are break-out rooms where we can watch close-up routines, big illusions, and parlor magic.

"What's parlor magic," Marc innocently asked.

"It's magic for about 10 or 20 people. Just a little more advanced than close-up work, but lots of fun."

"Can't wait," Marc smiled.

"There are also rooms where you can buy magic tricks and books," Ray winked.

"Great, I brought some of my birthday money. If I see a trick I like, I may buy it."

"I'm sure they would be more than happy to accommodate you," Uncle Ray chuckled.

At the actual event, Marc was in awe of the crowd and venue. As promised, it was a huge occurrence. He was also impressed with how many of the magicians on the floor knew his uncle, indicating that the man was a little more famous than the lad had ever imagined.

After shaking hands with many compeers, Ray led Marc to the auditorium to witness opening night. It was not disappointing. Seigfreid and Roy did several routines. The climax of the show was the disappearance of a large white lion. which had been put in a cage and covered with a sheet. When it was removed, voila! The cat was gone! Upon covering the cage again, the magical duo revealed that the big cat was alive and well and led him to the apron of the stage. Not surprisingly, there was roaring applause.

The next day, Marc attended the close-up show and learned many amazing affects with cards and small props. He also enjoyed the parlor show, which showcased tricks that he could perform in front of small groups. The biggest surprise is that he enjoyed the break-out group on mentalism. Here, he was asked by the Amazing Kreskin to join him as a willing subject. One affect was called "Red Hammer." Here, Kreskin asked a series of questions: What's your favorite Christmas meal? What date is Valentine's Day? What plant comes after earth? What are hamburgers made of? Can you think of a color and a tool?

Marc answered that last question: Red…Hammer. With that, Kreskin turned over a paper he had written in advance. Yes, it revealed Red Hammer….along with a picture of the object.

Kreskin did a few more affects with Marc, and invited the small group to give the young man a round of applause for helping him.

After those two break-out groups, a thrilled Marc went to the magic store and bought several books on magic. He also brought a few affects. They were mostly close-up or parlor effects. Nothing too big to bring on a return flight.

As a finale, Uncle Ray and Marc watched the closing stage act of David Copperfield, who performed "13." Here, 13 audience members are brought on stage and seated on a platform. It is then covered with a curtain. Copperfield tries to prepare the audience that they will be watching a miracle. After a few minutes, he pulls back the curtain and reveals that all 13 audience members have disappeared.

Just for a kicker, Copperfield looks for them in the audience… and points to them at the back of the auditorium. When he asks them to wave, all 13 do and Copperfield bows to a loud applause,

So thrilled with his weekend in Las Vegas, Marc effusively thanked his Uncle Ray for bringing him and exposing him to the magic arts. All the way home, he sat next to his uncle, read his new books and practiced with his new decks of cards. His uncle, beaming, felt great that he had a disciple, who truly enjoyed sleight-of-hand and entertaining people. Fact is, Marco the Magnificent (as he decided to call himself) would enjoy it for many years to come.

Chapter 8

Marc definitely enjoyed his new friends from the magic society. Bobby, Carlos and Barry were so envious that Marc had the opportunity to actually attend a big-time magic convention. They each had their particular favorite tricks, but given Marc's experience in Las Vegas and his purchases of books and gimmicks, his repertoire was a little more advanced. So what? He enjoyed having a willing audience of true magic aficionados. He also loved the exposure to new affects that his friends were more than pleased to share.

Unfortunately, he and his magic friends could only get together about once a month, when the Society of Young Magicians had their regular meetings. None of the young men lived close to each other. Of course, there was the telephone, but it wasn't so effective for the tadaa of a magic trick.

Marc had made friends at Hamilton High, but those boys were mostly interested in sports, weekend movies, and of course, girls. A few times, he tried to show them tricks he had learned. However, most of them only had a polite interest in the craft. It was like sharing artwork or short stories with high school kids. Not exactly a ticket to easy popularity.

Marc had learned this lesson a few years earlier. Only a few classmates ever had the interest or patience to view a trick's build-up and ultimate reveal. Grown-ups seemed to get a kick out of his magic, and some girls actually rather enjoyed the surprise and giggles of a trick, perhaps because it was so different from the usual jock-talk that many high school boys loved to discuss nonstop.

Even so, Pat Foley was always one of the few classmates that seemed to get a genuine kick out of his tricks. Even in their earliest days together, she would react to his magic with wide-eyed appreciation. Importantly, she never asked him how an effect was done. Consequently, Marc was always confident that she would never reveal his secrets, since she really never knew any of them.

A very popular girl, Pat had plenty of friends in high school. Perhaps it was her good looks. More likely, it was her outgoing personality. Even in the recesses between classes, she was often surrounded by classmates. Lunchtime was usually a rotating picnic, with invitees changing every day.

At this particular lunchtime, Marc happened to in the line just behind Pat. Consequently, she asked her favorite magician to join her group at the table.

"What's new? How's tricks?" she asked him.

"Not much. I've been practicing," he admitted. Between bites, he asked her if she had been singing lately.

"A little. Although my dad wants me to just concentrate on schoolwork. Enough with the music," he says.

"Yeah, but you're so good. It's a talent. You can't put that on the backburner."

"I don't. I still go to my voice lessons," she shrugged.

After comparing notes about classes, and some chitchat with her friends, they were finally at the table all by themselves. "Marc, show me a new trick," she said, rubbing her hands together in anticipation.

'Wanna see one?" Marc gleefully asked.

"Show me. Amaze me," she answered.

With a smile, Marco the Magnificent brought out a deck of cards. This is a miracle I call the blacks and the reds. And you're going to end of doing most of the work."

He then looked inside the deck and took out the ten of spades. "A black card," he said. Next to it, he then picked different card—the three of hearts. He then proudly announced "a red card."

He took the deck in his left hand and prepared her for the effect. "All the cards in the deck are either red or black. I don't know which is which, and you don't either. But I am asking you to FEEL in your mind which card is which color. Don't look. Just put them face down in a row. If you think it's black, put it here. If you think it's red, put it here. "

One by one, Pat began to put the cards down in a row. At first she put them down slowly, as if concentrating on the hidden colors.

Some to the left. Some to the right. After about ten cards, she began to speed up a little and started putting them down with confidence.

After a while, Marc stopped her. "Wait. Pat, I get the feeling you are not concentrating enough. Let's switch things up a little." He then took the deck after she was about half way through and switched the lead card. Below the black card and the face down cards, Marc then placed a red card. On the red card row, he then placed a black card. "Put the rest of the cards down one by one, face down. If you think it's red, now put it here. If you think it's black, put it in this row now."

Satisfied that she had put the cards in the right rows, Pat looked at Marc.

He then pointed to the black ten of spades at the top of the row. "Let's see if you got any other black cards in that row." One by one, she turned over the cards and—lo and behold—they were all black.

"Now, check those cards under the three of hearts," he advised her. As she reached for the row, Marc took two other rows on the right, and turned over the face down cards. Again, all the reds were together and all the blacks flowed from the lead black card.

Pat looked at the color-coordinated rows in utter amazement. She even screamed with laughter, and applauded her achievement.

Marc also acted as if he was surprised. "How did you do that?" he teased her.

Acting the role, she said, "I am not allowed to tell you. A famous magician once told me that a magician is never allowed to reveal his (or her) secrets.

"That's true." Marc agreed and gave her a thumbs up. As he remembered from their grade school days together, that's one big reason they became fast friends.

Still looking at the rows of red and black cards, Pat simply shook here head with amazement.

Just about then the bell rang. It was time for everyone in the cafeteria to return to class. Both Pat and Marc walked out the cafeteria buoyed by the experience they just had together.

Marc trailed her and was privately quite proud that he had mastered this illusion. Instinctlively, he wished he could share more with his good friend, Pat.

Chapter 9

On Thursday evening, Pat had her regularly scheduled voice lesson.

Her mother was always enthusiastic about her daughter's interest in music.

As a mom who knew how to play the piano well, she had accompanied her daughter ever since she could carry a tune. They were usually pop songs, since these were the favored tunes of Mrs. Foley—Carole King, Whitney Houston, Maria Carey, Celine Dion, Dionne Warwick and others.

Part of the appeal of this genre was that Pat's dad also derived some pleasure from these melodies. As a journalist and an avid reader, he was not a music aficionado. However, he occasionally enjoyed the songs he could hear on the radio.

Pat had many books of sheet music, and would ordinarily bring several to her voice teacher, a 20-something woman named Michelle, who had been in musicals and occasionally sang in New York clubs. She was a good judge of talent, and truly believed her young student had loads of it. She could easily carry any tune and build a decent crescendo.

In view of her recent get-together with Marc, she wanted to explore some songs about Friendship. She brought along the sheet music for "You've Got a Friend," "That's What Friends Are For," and "You've Got a Friend in Me."

"I love all of these songs," Michelle exclaimed. "Especially the Carole King classic. And wow, I love the fact that they are all on the same subject. Let's start with the first one."

As usual, Michelle would take a few minutes to learn the chords on the piano. She would then ask Pat to sing along softly to get a feel for how the piano melody and voice went together. After a few passes, the teacher would then invite her student to give it a go.

Today, she decided to take a different path.

The teacher said, "Since this is story of friendship, before you begin your rendition, let's spend a few minutes talking about that very thing.

"What's it take to be a friend?" Michelle asked.

After a minute, Pat answered, "Appreciating the other person's strengths."

"Anything else," Michelle wondered.

"Forgiving their weaknesses," Pat answered and saw that Michelle was motioning for more.

Pat continued. "Being there for the other person—come rain or come shine. Just enjoying the moment with another person. Feeling so at ease."

Michelle was nodding her head at her student's thoughts. "Those are all good. Now let's think of this specific song. You, my dear, have a pitch perfect voice. But I want to elevate your performances to the next level. Don't even think of imitating Carole King's voice. Just be yourself."

"I will," Pat responded. I couldn't sound like Carole King, if I wanted to."

"And I don't want you to. Just sound like you," her teacher agreed. "Now I'll tell you one other secret that I use when I perform in a musical or in a club. I think of someone specific. And I sing that song to him or her. That's the real trick to putting emotion into every rendition."

"That's the trick?" Pat asked with a smile.

"That's the trick." Michelle agreed. "Let's give it a go. Ready?"

Pat nodded and Michelle started playing the introduction. When she hit the part when the vocal hits, Pat sang right on cue. She started it softly, but gathered steam as the song progressed. After the bridge, she upped the emotion and built to a crescendo, only to resolve the song quietly and sincerely.

When she finished, Michelle applauded and took out a hanky. Fact is, her eyes had welled up with the amazing rendition. "That's as good as anything I have ever heard from you. I'd say you are ready to perform in a nightclub."

Pat bowed, but demurred. "I've got a long way to go before I go to a club."

"Not really," Michelle disagreed. "But in the weeks to come, we'll continue working on songs with all those thoughts in mind.

Pat smiled and looked at her watch. "Oh my. It's time to go. My mom is probably outside."

Michelle waved goodbye and truly believed she had a very talented, potential star in her midst.

Chapter 10

Seeing the progress that his nephew was making, Uncle Ray thought it was perhaps time for Marc to take the next big step.

Ever since their trip to Las Vegas, Marc had graduated to more challenging illusions. Some had been the result of props he had bought. More of them came from the magic books he had purchased and carefully studied.

He practiced them often at home and with his friends at their regularly scheduled Society of Young Magician meetings. His parents could easily see the progress and his young friends were always amazed at Marc's dexterity and delivery.

Ray thought his young understudy was ready to join the adult group, which included many professionals and long-time members. This group was called The Society of American Magicians, and it met monthly in Manhatttan. It would require a sponsor (Uncle Ray) and a true audition.

"You think I am really ready?" Marc asked his uncle.

"I do. But I'm not talking about joining the group tonight. You should take a few months and practice a short routine. It doesn't have to be any longer than eight or ten minutes, but it's got to be flawless. Think of which two tricks you might want to perform and do them over and over again until they are second nature to you."

"I will," Marc promised. "And I'll show them to you many, many times.

You'll probably get tired of seeing them."

"Never," Uncle Ray answered. "I love watching your magic."

Marc looked through his bag of tricks and books and tried many in front of the mirror. Some were flashy. Some required patter. Some were better done in silence, or perhaps to accompanying music.

He automatically eliminated many of his close-up effects. He loved this style of magic, but felt that it would require his judges crowding in front of a table in front of him. Also, he began to believe that any nervousness on his part would show itself in such a setting--and he believed there is nothing worse than a magician with shaky hands. Nope. He decided it would be better to try parlor tricks. That way, his audience could stay comfortably in their seats, and he could even walk back and forth, forward or back, if he needed to.

Once he had settled on a routine, he shared it with his uncle, who agreed that his choices might make a nice impression. "The key thing is the presentation. Practice, practice until you are very relaxed. Figure out what you want to say to open the show and close the show….and you don't have to talk every minute of the show. Sometimes, a little music can add to the mystery---especially for a trick like Zombie."

Marc agreed and practiced this effect to music. It's a beautiful trick that involves a silk and silver ball that seems to float behind it and above it. He spent hours choreographing the trick to a instrumental track from the Steve Miller Band. It was called "Fly Like an Eagle."

When he showed it to his uncle, Ray congratulated him on handling of the props, but argued that the music was wrong. "It's too modern for this audience. There will be a lot of old guys in the audience. I don't think they will recognize music from the Steve Miller Band. Try to find something from Sinatra or Dean Martin or Rosemary Clooney. Someone from that era."

Marc nodded and understood. He explored several alternatives and finally settled on one. With much rehearsal, he felt that it would make a wonderful impression.

His other trick—a thing called the Linking Rings—was probably better with live patter. It required him to explain to the audience what was about the happen right before their eyes.

After several trial runs in front of his Uncle, he began to feel more and more comfortable with his routine.

Ray suggested that they aim for the Society of American Magician meeting a month from now.

On the evening of his actual performance, Uncle Ray introduced his the young man. "Ladies and Gentlemen, I would like to introduce you to Marco the Magnificent—a name he picked up when we attended the convention in Las Vegas. He is my nephew, and he practices all the time. I think he would make a wonderful addition to our great group of pros. Marc?" he called out to the lad to take the stage.

Marc brought a small piece of luggage on stage and opened it. He then addressed the audience. "Good evening. It's a real thrill to meet all of you. My name is Marc Obie, but as my Uncle Ray calls me "Marco the Magnificient." Hopefully, you'll agree."

He then reached into his bag and pulled out six metal rings. They were each about ten inches in diameter.

He proudly announced, "Six rings. Let's count them together. One. Two. Three. Four. Five. Six." As he did so, he held the entire stack in his left hand and let them fall into his right hand one by one.

"Let's start with three of these rings." He then took two of them and rubbed the edges together. "Watch," he told the audience. The two rings miraculously linked together. He rotated them both and showed that they were locked. He then took the third ring.

"Let's make this more complicated. He then rubbed that one up the conjoined two and showed that all three were now linked. With some surprise, he then said, "I don't even know how I do that."

The audience chuckled.

He then put the three linked rings up his left arm and took the remaining rings in his right hand. One after the next after the next he linked the remaining three.

He completed the effect by putting all the rings together, and counting them as separate. In conclusion, he held all six rings above his head and ended the routine by saying "The linking rings, according to Marco."

There was a nice round of applause, and Marc thanked the crowd.

"But I'm not done yet," Marc said. He then brought out a small musical recorder and hit "play." As he did so, an instrumental of the Sinatra hit 'Come fly with me.' began to play. Marc reached in his luggage and pulled out a colorful silk scarf. He showed both sides of the silk.

Then perfectly coordinated with the music, he held the silk and showed a bulge coming from the center. It moved the silk to the right, and he followed along. Then to the left. And then—tadaa—the big reveal. As he held both sides of the silk, a silver ball began to float on the top.

Again, synchronized with Sinatra classic, the silver ball seemed to bounce on the top of the silk. Eventually, it gradually disappeared, and Marco again showed both sides of the colorful silk and placed all his materials back in the small bag.

Perfectly timed, the music faded and Marco took a bow. Again, there was applause--this time with a little more gusto.

Marc bowed and spoke to the audience. "Folks, thanks for your attention and your interest. Hope you enjoyed my little show. Hope to see you again soon."

With that, he walked off the stage and exited the room as his Uncle Ray had told him to do. Ray followed him out the room, and shook his hand. He then said that the group needed to vote and he needed to join them. "I don't think this will take long," Ray predicted.

After about five minutes, Jerry Borman, the president of the Society of American magicians opened the door and said hello to the young man, who pacing back and forth.

"Congratulations," Mr. Borman said with a smile. "You are officially a member of S.A.M. Come with me and meet your new compeers."

Marc raised a triumphantly raised fist in the air and once in the room, shook the hands of all his fellow members. He would never remember all their names, but with Ray's help, he would get to know all of them soon enough.

On the way home, Ray told him that several of the older magicians particularly liked his Zombie routine along with the "Come Fly with me," music.

"You did great," said. "You know, you're their youngest member, and the vote was unanimous." Once home, his mom and dad gave him a big hug and told him that they were so proud of their son.

Elated, Marco wanted to share the news with the world, but he could only think of one person to tell. Her name was Pat Foley. He looked at the clock on the kitchen wall and discovered that it was already 10:45 p.m. Too late. He decided that the good news could wait til tomorrow.

Chapter 11

On the bus the next morning, Marc sat next to Pat and beamed.

After a few minutes on the road, he teased that a big event had happened for him last night.

"Oh, tell me," she pleaded.

"I went to the grown-up Society of American magicians meeting last night. My uncle recommended me for membership, and I had to audition with a ten-minute routine. I passed the test."

"What do you mean?" Pat asked.

"While I waited outside, the group voted on me, and I was accepted! I was voted in as a member. It's a big deal. They're all pros… and I am the youngest full-time member."

"That's just great!" She gushed.

"I almost called you last night to tell you, but it was too late," he sad.

"You can call me anytime. I want to hear all about it. What tricks you showed them? How did it feel? How nervous were you? "

"Very."

"I want to hear all about it at lunch. Sit next to me. If I get through the cafeteria line first, I'll save you a seat….and vice versa."

"Deal."

Marc tried to concentrate on his morning classes, but in all honesty, he couldn't wait to tell his friend Pat all about the performance.

He told her that he had rehearsed for months for this opportunity. Then he described the effect of the linking rings.

"Not an easy trick," he admitted, "but I wanted to show the long-time members that I could perform a classic."

"I assume it went well," she probed.

"It went perfectly…but my next trick clinched the deal. It's an effect called Zombie, and what happens is that I hold a silk and then a silver ball miraculously appears behind it and then floats on the top of it. "

"Wow."

"Yeah, but the best part was what the audience heard. Instead of describing every move, I played a piece of instrumental music and performed it to the audio. The crowd went nuts."

"You actually played music?"

"No, just a tape of the music. It was 'Come Fly with me," by Frank Sinatra. No words on my part. Just a beautiful effect set to music."

"Oh, I love that," she clapped her hands.

"I thought you would, knowing how much you love music and how good you are at it."

"Music and magic…and interesting combination," she said nodding her head.

"Yeah, my uncle suggested it, and then I listened to all kinds of tunes before I found the right one."

Pat gave him a private applause and agreed. "That's exactly the process I am using in my voice lessons. I listen to tons of records and find one that fits my mood."

"Fun, isn't it?" he smiled.

"It's a blast!" she agreed

He was glad to hear that she was continuing with her performance interests. "You're so good at singing," he told her. "But I feel like I did most of the talking during this lunch. I want to hear all about your progress with music."

"I'll tell you all about it," she promised. "Let's do this lunch thing every Monday, and I'll fill you in on my next steps."

"I can't wait." Marc answered, just as the bell rang to return to class. As he walked to class, he did so with a little pep in his step, given the encouragement Pat had given him. He vowed to himself that he would definitely return the favor to his talented friend.

Chapter 12

In the ensuing months, Pat and Marc enjoyed a weekly lunch together and often compared notes on their artistic pursuits. It was definitely a sympatico relationship. However, it was not a romantic relationship.

Each of them was busy with academic workloads and their widening circles of friends. However, unlike a lot of other students who only attend class and just escape the grind on weekends, both had a true extracurricular passion.

Somewhat inspired by Marc's creative progress in the field of magic, Pat took a renewed interest in music. She truly appreciated Michelle's lesson about making her songs more personal and meaningful to the listener.

She also admired the fact that Marc had taken the initiative to propel his talent more publicly. Privately, she told herself that it was time to take her singing beyond a middle-school talent show. Yes, she had been doing so in her voice lessons. But those were remote, removed experiences.

At about that time, she saw a flyer on the bulletin board for the upcoming high school musical auditions. Despite the fact that she was only a junior and had never been in an actual musical, she was definitely intrigued by the prospect of giving it a try.

The musical was "Grease,"—a big song-and-dance extravaganza that was made famous in the movie version by John Travolta and Olivia Newton-John. That night, she rented the movie and watched it in her bedroom after her homework.

It was eye-opening. Unlike the goody, two-shoes imagery that many associated with Pat, this was a story that had rough edges—forbidden love, unwanted pregnancies, gangs, jealousy, you name it.

It also had some great music, including "Look at me, I'm Sandra Dee." "Hopelessly Devoted to You." And "You're the One that I want." Unfortunately, it also had great dancing. This was not her forte… but deep down, she instinctively believed that the ability to sing was probably more important than jazz dancing.

In quiet preparation for the audition, she told her voice teacher about the upcoming musical. Michelle encouraged her to definitely give it a try. "We'll practice some great audition songs, As a matter of fact, you already have many…but we'll practice more."

Pat thought that perhaps she should audition with her version of ""Hopelessly devoted to you."

"Nope," Michelle answered. "Too obvious. Too risky. Besides, the director will want to shape this song in the image they already have in their mind."

"Got any suggestions?"

"That's a musical about falling in love…and it all starts with friendship," Michelle answered. Fortunately, we have explored that turf.

I think that perhaps you should try the Dionne Warwick hit, "That's what friends are for." It's a love song like "Hopelessly Devoted to You,"….but at least it will impress the casting director and let him or her "see you" in the role. "sessions. As advised by Michelle, she would imagine singing the song to someone special. Occasionally, when she would take the bus with Marco, she would find herself humming the melody.

On the afternoon of the audition, she waited patiently until her name was called and then entered the room, carrying the sheet music. As the pianist began to play the intro, she closed her eyes and imagined the recipient.

As then she began singing about the fact that she "never thought she'd feel this way." The melody built and so did her voice. However, it was always with a smile and a true hope that thing would work out.

When she reached the finale, the casting director asked for her details—name, phone number, etc. Also… "Have you ever been in a musical?"

"I've been in talent shows," Pat answered. "But hopefully, this will be my first musical."

"Well, you did well. We will post the call-backs next Wednesday. By the way, if you do get a call back, I might want to hear you sing, "Hopelessly Devoted to You." Are you familiar with that song?

"I am," Pat answered.

Good luck, the casting director said, and waved goodbye.

Michelle, the voice coach, was delighted to hear this news. "That means you wowed them with your audition," she said. "OK, let's kill them with "Hopelessly devoted…"

In anticipation, Pat had listened to the song many times from the movie video. She had even rehearsed it with her mom at the piano at home.

"Now don't forget, Pat. Visualize someone. See him. Think of him. Sing to him. After all, you are hopeless devoted to him."

As she had done in the initial audition, Pat closed her eyes and imagined her secret heart throb When the pianist began to play the intro, she sat on a stool and looked to the heavens. Then she began to softly sing "There's just no getting over you," and emoting about feeling alone with a broken heart.

As the music began to build, she moved off the stool and began to feel swept with emotion—"out of her head," as she sang. At the end of the song, she smiled at the pianist and the director and politely thanked them for the chance to sing in front of them.

"That was impressive," the director said. "Can you dance?"

"At a dance, I can dance," she answered as noncommittally as possible. "But most of my training has been in voice."

"I would say to your parents, it is money well spent. We will post the cast next Monday. I wish you the best."

In the early evening, she met with her parents and told them she thought she had done well. After that, she called Michelle, her voice teacher, and went into more detail about every minute of the audition.

She then looked at the clock, and saw that it was approaching 10 p.m.

Recalling that she had told Marc that he could call anytime, she decided to take her own advice and dial his cellphone.

"Are you still up?" she asked.

"Yes!"

"I just auditioned for the musical *Grease*, and I think I did well," she proclaimed.

"Tell me all about it," he answered.

She began to describe every minute, but then suggested she fill him in more fully over lunch.

"I am proud of you for having the courage to do this." he said

"Me, too," she answered, and soon closed her eyes with a smile on her face.

Chapter 13

On the following Monday, Pat looked on the school bulletin board the first thing in the morning. Nothing was posted there about the cast of "Grease."

As a result, she simply went to her classes and tried to keep her mind on the academic subjects. It wasn't easy. She found herself reliving her audition performance and fantasizing about the chorus numbers.

After lunch, she went back to board to see if it had any good news. Same blank space. Finally, when the last school bell rang, Pat went back to the board, and discovered that there was a crowd around one particular sheet of paper.

Yes, it was the announced cast of "Grease." A few kids left with a disappointed look on their face. Obviously, they had not made the cut. When Pat got close enough to read the list, she screamed with joy.

The lead role of Danny would be played by Johnny Tucci. The key role of Sandy would be played by Pat Foley. The other actors of major parts were also named (as was the chorus), but to be perfectly honest, Pat quit reading after seeing her name. She did look to the bottom of the sheet and saw that the first rehearsal would be Wednesday after school in the theatre. There was another involuntary yelp from Pat.

On a cloud, she raced to the bus outside which was quickly filling up with classmates. Once she got inside, she saw one empty seat—next to Marc. She raced down the aisle and told gleefully told him the great news.

He was legitimately happy for her. He knew she had true talent. It was nice to have that verified by a casting director and for all her high school classmates.

On the first night of rehearsal, Pat went the theatre a few minutes early and introduced herself to other cast members. She actually recognized Johnny Tucci, a senior who played the lead role of Curly in last year's production of "Oklahoma." Great voice. A little tall next to her, but it would probably look right for a play like "Grease."

On this initial night, Gina Brown, the director, introduced every member of the cast and asked them to stand. She then told them that over the next few nights, she would be giving an overview of the entire musical and play every song. "No one will be required to sing right now. There will be plenty of time for that," she said.

She then promised individual coaching in a few side rooms for the roles of Danny, Sandy, Rizzo, Frenchy, and Kenickie. "While this goes on, we will have chorus rehearsals on the main stage," she said.

"I have a rehearsal schedule for everyone," the director said and passed them out. "This will be the shortest one. Every other one will run about three tours …until 6:30 p.m. No rehearsals on the weekends…

until the one before dress rehearsals. It's a chance for everyone to rest their voices and their dancing feet. For now, let me congratulate you all, and wish you a great evening, and a great eventual performance of 'Grease,'

When the crowd began to disband, Johnny did approach Pat and congratulate her on getting the role of Sandy. "I don't know if we ever met. Were you in the show last year?"

"Nope," she answered. "But I am really looking forward to this year's show."

Johnny smiled at her and agreed. "I'm sure we will be great together," he added. "I've got a car waiting for me now, and I've got to go, so... see you tomorrow."

"Manana," Pat answered and waved goodbye. She then went out to the parking lot and got in her mom's car. As soon as she get in the front seat, she happily squealed and gave her mother the rehearsal schedule. She also asked her mom to pin it on the wall in the kitchen so everyone would know her late nights.

"Good start?" her mom winked

"Great start!" she agreed and giggled.

Chapter 14

On their first true rehearsal night, Gina had scheduled Pat and Johnny in a side room.

She addressed them both with her opening comments. "I wanted to start out with you two in the same room, since so much of this musical depends on the relationship between Sandy and Danny. My guess is you have seen the movie or maybe even a live musical of "Grease." As you might know, you are an interesting couple. In some ways, you don't have a lot in common…but as the story unfolds, you become closer together. Johnny, you start out as "greaser" guy who thinks he is too cool for words. Pat, as the story begins, you are a sweet stranger. You both meet at the beach during the summer months, and bit by bit, things begin to click…despite the jealousy and "smart ass" comments of your classmates.

"Let me tell you why I cast you both. Johnny, I directed you last year in "Oklahoma," so I had a good idea of what you could do. But that was a "nice guy" role. This guy, Danny Zuko, is sometimes a real jerk, so you can't always be so lovable on stage. I want you to grow out your hair. Get used to carrying a comb and combing it straight back, like Travolta did. Oh, and Johnny…there's a lot of dancing in this role.

I want you to spend a good amount of time with choreographer, so it looks natural on stage."

"I saw the movie, Johnny answered. "The dancing looks cool."

"And it will be in our musical," Gina answered.

She then turned to Pat and addressed her. "Sandy Olsen, welcome," the director said. "I didn't work with you last year, so you are a fresh face…which a big part of the role. Few people at Rydel High (the high school in the musical) knew you. And that's the appeal you have for our audience, as well. I will say one more thing, Pat. I was absolutely blown away by your voice and your ability to connect emotionally with the audition songs you sang. Have you heard her sing, Johnny?

"Not yet," he admitted.

"Well, you are in for a treat," Gina said. She then reached for her pile of sheet music.

"Let's start this with a few solo songs, so you can get used to each other's voices. Johnny, you go first. This song is called "Sandy." It's sung solo by Danny as he walks through the aisles of a drive-in movie theatre. It isn't exactly a love song, Johnny. It's actually about a break-up. See, Sandy decides that maybe Danny is not such a good fit with her, so she says adios.

"Now, this upsets Danny—partly because he thinks there may be something there between the two of you. But the bigger reason is Danny has a big ego. He doesn't like the fact that his friends may now think he's not such a winner. Hey, he can't get the girl…so this makes him sad on a very egotistical level. It ends with Danny looking at the sky and saying "Why? Why? Why?" Let's give it a try. On the first run-through, just try to get the melody. Once you get used to it, you can then add all kinds of emotion."

As Gina cued the piano player, Johnny began to sing along quietly, just so he could get a sense of the melody. After a few attempts, he upped the volume a little and tried to get the swing of the tune.

"Good," the director said. "It's not an easy song,..and it's not that well known, but you will definitely get the hang of it."

"Yeah, it's an odd song. I've watched the musical a few times, and it doesn't stick in my mind automatically."

"It will," the director promised, "with a little practice." Gina then handed out a different sheet music song to Pat. "I know you know this song, since you sang it in your call-back audition. But I'm in the mood to hear "Hopeless devoted to you," again. There will not be much dancing with this song. I envision you singing it on a porch. Let's give it a go."

When the pianist started playing, Pat closed her eyes and imagined the object of her affection. Once she had a picture of Marc in her mind, she began singing about a distant love. It was convincing.

As the song concluded, Johnny sat there wide-eyed and even applauded. "Wow, that was wonderful!"

"Of course, it was," Gina beamed. "Why else would I have cast her as your leading lady?"

Pat was blushing, but appreciated the compliments.

Gina looked at her watch. "We don't have too much more time, but now that you both know each other's voices, let's try a duet. A beautiful one from this musical is called "Summer nights." It's a reflection on your times together during those beach days…and nights.

The director gave the sheet music to both of them. "No need to 'sell' this song emotionally. I just want you both to get used to the melody and enjoy a first crack at this song that involves both of your voices. First, we'll do it slowly….and then the next time, a little more engaged. And then, we should be about out of time."

As the director noted, this is a song about their times together, when they meet at the beach during the summer, and fell for each other. On these quick run-throughs, it was a little hard to get the back-and-forth just right, but it was a good start. "That's good. That's enough for one day," Gina said. "Tomorrow, you get a day off from these solos and duets. I want you to stay close to the chorus stage, and get a feeling for how the dance numbers will go."

"That's great," Pat answered and started gathering her things.

Johnny followed right behind her caught up with her in the hallway.

"Damn, you've got a good voice," he said. "This is going to be an amazing musical."

"I hope so," Pat nodded.

"Have you heard Rizzo's or Frenchy's voices yet?

"Nope."

"They're good. Between all four of us, this is amazing. And tomorrow, we get to see how the dance numbers will go."

"A lot of them are just you and the guys in the gang," she prayed.

"Yeah, a lot are. But we will have a few numbers too, and that will be fun."

"I am sure it will."

When they exited the school, Pat saw her mom's car and asked him to join her. "I just want to introduce you to my mom." When she arrived, she said, "Mother, this is my Johnny Tucci, my leading man."

He extended his hand to Mrs. Foley, and remarked that the young woman had an amazing voice—both in terms of range and emotion."

"Yeah, well she practices enough."

"I'll bet."

"You need a ride to your home?" she asked Johnny.

"No, I already have my driver's license, and tonight, I was able to use my family's car. So I'm fine." He then waved and said, "Pat, I'll see you tomorrow."

"Can't wait."

Chapter 15

After weeks of rehearsal, the show was definitely taking shape and showing dramatic signs of improvement.

Not surprisingly, the dance numbers were the hardest to perfect. Part of it was the precision of jazz dancing in a group of eight or ten people. If one person is off, the audience's eye inevitably focuses on the mistake. Fortunately, for the guy's numbers, there was a fair amount of finger-snapping and jumping back and forth. It wasn't exactly ballet.

The women's routines had slightly more finesse, but these dances too had a gang-like personality. Pat was pleased she didn't really have a starring presence in the dance numbers. True, as a major character, she couldn't hide in the background, but she didn't really have a solo center stage role in terms of dance. For her, it amounted to a lot of skipping on stage and sliding back and forth.

Johnny did have more of a solo presence in his dance numbers, and seemed to have a good knack for combining steps with guy songs. Examples: "Greased lightning," and "We Go Together."

There was one number where she did share a dance with the lead character Danny. It's a high-energy prance towards the end of the show. In it, Pat demonstrates that she has evolved to appeal to the male gang members. Instead of being costumed in those pretty dresses, she is now attired in leather pants and a sexy blouse.

In this number, she is dancing with Danny, but in his sleeveless T-shirt, tight jeans and white sox, he definitely takes center stage. Also, her choreography is principally about hopping or skipping in front of him. Not exactly difficult for any girl who grew up doing hopscotch.

Perhaps the most memorable song in the entire musical is the curtain closing finale. It's called "You're the One that I want." In it, Danny chases her through a chorus of dancers and ends the show by catching her and closing with a big hug and a kiss.

It took a little work since it involved so many people on stage. However, it is definitely a boffo ending.

In the closing weeks and long nights of rehearsals, Johnny was able to drive his family's car. He gladly offered to give Pat a ride home since they didn't live too far apart. They had good chemistry on stage, which was evident to all.

On one of those nights, Johnny stopped in the park, looked at the moon, and wanted to discuss their favorite parts of the show. Both agreed that "Summer Nights" was definitely up there.

"There's one part of the number that I'm not sure quite clicks," Johnny volunteered.

"Which part?" Pat innocently asked.

"Our kiss at the end of the song. I'm not sure it's convincing,"

This baffled her, since she thought the ending of the song was good.

"I think we should practice that kiss," Johnny quietly said. "Let's rehearse it a few times here." He then snuggled next to her and put her arm around her shoulder. Slowly and gently, he pressed his lips against hers.

"Yeah, I think that's better, " he said. "Let's try it again." He snuggled next to her and gave a longer kiss.

It's not that Pat didn't know what was going on. She had always been a smart girl, and it didn't take a genius to appreciate the emotion. In fact, she decided to return the favor, and make the next move. She rubbed her hand on his cheek and then made the romantic move.

Again, and again…the two of them enjoyed the feeling of closeness.

Finally, after about 15 minutes, Pat suggested that she really had to get home. "If we need to rehearse it further, perhaps we can do it again tomorrow night," she kidded him.

"Yeah, absolutely. We are definitely getting there," he said and smiled all the way to getting her home.

Over the next several nights of rehearsals, they perfected that kiss after school, accompanied by hugs and touches.

It quietly affected her performance. When she sang "Hopelessly devoted to you," she had always closed her eyes and envisioned Marc. In the last few days, that visual changed. She started to fantasize Johnny. In a sense, their after-hours embraces in the car were hard to forget. Also, it was easier to stay in character.

Spurred by this, the final rehearsals were quite a thrill. Even Gina congratulated Pat on her performances. "It seems you have really found your character. Very believable."

On the day of the final dress rehearsal, Marc joined her on the morning school bus. "I hear the play is great," he told her as he sat next to her.

"I think it's pretty good," she understated.

"I'll bet you are fantastic in it," he gushed, and then said. "I haven't seen you much lately. I've missed you."

"Well, I've been tied up day and night. I barely have time to do my homework."

He knew that feeling from when he was preparing for a show, but he also wanted to reassure her that he was in her corner. "I'm going to come opening night. Can't wait to hear you sing again."

"Well, I hope you like it."

"I'm gonna love it," he corrected her and both exited the bus to go to their different classes.

Opening night was played for a packed theatre. Often, the audience interrupted the performance with loud applause after energetic numbers. As Marc could tell, Danny (Johnny) and Sandy (Pat) seemed to garner the biggest hoorays.

At the end of the show, they each had many standing ovations, and bowed together holding hands.

Marc thoroughly enjoyed it, and was particularly swept away by Pat's performance.

After the show, he hung out to give her a big hug and tell her how great she was. "That was absolutely stunning," he told her. "You have such an amazing gift."

"Aww, you're too nice," she answered.

"Wanna go get a soda or a pizza at Lombardo's?" he innocently asked, looking forward to complimenting her on each specific number.

"Damn, I can't. We've got a big cast party tonight, and I promised I would join them." As she said it, she motioned to a few others not to leave without her.

"I totally understand," Marc said, and watched her run off to meet Johnny. The couple walked out of the theatre arm in arm.

Chapter 16

The romance extended beyond the final curtain.

Pat and Johnny started going to restaurants, movies, and parties together after the closing of "Grease." In some ways, it was a typecasting thrill for their friends. On the stage, it looked as if they belonged together, and it didn't take much to fantasize about them dancing together at drive-ins as Johnny had done when he was singing "Sandy" in the play.

True to form, he regularly wanted to "rehearse and practice" those kisses in the car after a date. Not surprisingly, sometimes he wanted more than a kiss. Pat was not accustomed to such next steps, but didn't really resist. She told herself that it was part of growing up, and moved things along to the next stage.

For the most part, Pat enjoyed this relationship, particularly in the first few months. Because there was a physical component, it felt more than just a figment of her imagination. However, because it was such a sudden click, she wondered if she should slow it down. And yet, as a novice in such progressions, she didn't quite know how.

Johnny didn't suffer such dilemmas. A year older than Pat (and more sexually advanced) he had been down this road before with other paramours. In truth, he had never been a one-woman guy…and even though he had a central casting leading lady at his side, he was still a wonderer at heart.

A few good-natured friends of Pat had warned her of that, and advised her not to fall head over heals. "He's a guy with a very short attention span," the cast member named Frenchy told her, "and he likes to keep his options open."

One other tell-tale sign: in her now resurrected voice lessons with Michelle, Pat had not always subliminally imagined Johnny in her love song prep. Now that the play was over, she found herself drifting back and forth between her former leading man and Marco the magnificent.

Marc had heard through the grapevine that his favorite gal now had a "main squeeze." He had suspected as much watching them leave hand in hand after the opening night of the musical. A few of his high school buddies knew that they were friends and wondered what he thought about the new liason.

Marc did a version of "no comment." Generally, he just walked away from these discussion. While he didn't want to seem too preoccupied with the gossip, he did honestly wonder if she was truly happy with this new relationship.

He had noticed lately that she had abandoned her usual lunch group, and rather than search for her from table to table, he choose to have his sandwich and soup with whoever was around him in the cafeteria line.

One of the advantages of being a magician is that it's a hobby that requires a lot of solo practice. In that regard, he was able to largely keep his mind on magic maneuvers on the table rather than the romantic entanglement of his friend.

Consequently, he did find himself privately practicing more and more card tricks.

Unfortunately, Pat did not have such an escape.

As more and more weeks went by, she did question Johnny's commitment to her. Instead of going out each night of the weekend, they began to date on only one night. True, it did give her more time to get more of her postponed homework assignments done. It also gave her more opportunities to go out with other guys, but she had no interest in being the young woman who went out with anybody.

Besides, the high school prom was coming up and she did want to go to that big event. Ever since the musical, she had assumed she and Johnny would go together and be the featured couple of the evening. Lately, she had begun to secretly question that.

On this weekend's date with Johnny, the subject came up… but not in the way that Pat would enjoy. During dinner at one of the local restaurants, Johnny mentioned that he wanted to have a "serious" conversation with Pat.

"It involves the upcoming prom," he admitted.

"Perhaps you know that I went last year with a classmate named Susie Brasfield. "

"No, I didn't know that," she answered. "I don't really follow your social dating history."

"Well, I did go with her, and spoke with her this week. Susie assumed we would go again to the prom this year."

"And?"

"And…I didn't really want to see her cry. So I told her yes last night….but I wanted to talk to you before you heard it from someone else."

After a pause, he added, "Were you thinking we would be prom partners this year?"

After a sip of her Coke, she said "Well, it had crossed my mind, but I figured you'd get around to asking me when the time was right."

"What I am telling you is that I am already committed."

"I hear you," she answered. "And I am no longer hungry. Let's get out of here. "

Johnny tried to hold her hand as he walked her to the car, but she resisted. On the drive to her home, Pat broke the silence. "You know what?' she began. "I think we had a good relationship on stage….but here in real life, I don't really think it's so hot."

When he pulled into her driveway, he tried to put his arm around her, "Aw, come on Pat. It's just one dance. Besides, it's not like we're going steady or anything."

"No, we are not," she answered. As a matter of fact, we are not going out at all anymore. This is goodbye." She then opened the car door and walked into her home.

She went straight to her room and let all this sink in. True she had enjoyed her time with Johnny, especially during the musical. However, for the most part, she was happy to call it quits. Once word got out that Johnny was taking his old girlfriend to the prom, she would feel like the second fiddle. No, it was far better for her to take responsibility for the break-up.

Less "poor girl," whispers in the school hallways. Less gossip about being jilted. All in all, less painful.

Of course, that left her dateless for the prom. A few guys were already spoken for. Also, it would take weeks for the word to get around that she might be available.

Rather than live in limbo, she decided to take matters in her own hands. Who says a guy has to do the asking? She decided that by the end of the upcoming week, she would have an ideal date for the prom.

Chapter 17

Marc had truly enjoyed his meetings with the Society of American Magicians. Despite being the youngest member, he genuinely felt accepted and encouraged in his pursuits.

At every meeting, one of the compeers would put on a brief presentation of his or her favorite tricks. Since they were all equal members, they would ordinarily explain the methodology of the effect. Of course, it was assumed that none of the magician spectators would "steal" the affect exactly as it was presented. No, that would not be cool. Of course, the trick could be adapted and translated to something new. That's what Marc often did. He would use the manipulation as a starting point, and create something that could be totally his own.

Of course, that same stricture did not exist in books and tricks he would buy online. Even so, Marc always tried his best to customize a trick so that it could be unique to him. Consequently, he had dozens of effects which he would keep in his shiny aluminum luggage. (On the top, he had painted Marco the Magnificent, so spectators would remember his name).

Trouble was, he didn't have that many spectators. True, he would share and practice most of his tricks with him mom and dad. He would also perfect the illusion with Uncle Ray, who always had good tips for him. As the young man's technique progressed in S.A.M meetings., he was also pleased that Ray would occasionally present and practice a new effect to Marc. Sometimes, he would even ask the young magician for an opinion. Do you think the build-up is enough? Should I tease the ending more? Marc was flattered that his uncle even wanted his opinion on these matters.

Marc, of course, wished he had a slightly wider audience. He had learned that not that many of his classmates wanted to see him practice new miracles at lunchtime or after school.

Of course, there had always been one exception: the young girl who had enjoyed his magical talent since grade school.

In the weeks after the musical, like most of his classmates, he had learned that Pat and Johnny were now a twosome. That explained why he rarely saw her on the bus before and after school and almost never viewed her in the cafeteria.

Somehow, inexplicably, that changed this week. He had begun to see her with her usual group of friends at lunchtime, Also, she would occasionally be on the same bus to his neighborhood at the end of the school day.

On one of those school days, he happened to be with her in the lunch line and she invited him to join her.

"Glad to," he answered and meant it. Truth is, he missed her, but didn't want to pry into her private social life. When he sat next to her at the table, she asked him what was new. He looked up to the ceiling and tried to think of something to say beyond the "same old, same old."

He finally thought of a brand-new, exciting event. "I'm getting my driver's license," he said.

"Wow, that's great."

"It's amazing," he agreed.

"Will you give me a ride sometime?"

"I would love to."

After a little more chitchat, the crowd around them at the table began to clear, and Pat reached out to touch his hand. "Hey, show me a new trick," she asked. "I've missed your talent to amaze me."

"Really?"

"Show me something new."

Marc took out a deck of cards and showed her that they were all different. He then cut the deck and asked her to take the top card. (it happened to be the five of hearts). "Don't show it to me," he said, "but here's what I want you to do: Sign the card. Then put it on the top of the deck."

As she did so, he shuffled the deck and held it in his hand. "Did any of your friends know the card you selected?" he teased.

She shook her head no.

He then took the pack and said "Watch!" With that, he threw the deck up to ceiling and watched all the cards fall down on the floor. No, not all! One card miraculously stuck to the ceiling! It was the five of hearts with her signature!

"Do you recognize that card?" he teased.

"Holy cow. That's one of the best tricks you have ever done," she remarked.

"Yeah, well…I have been saving it for you," he answered.

Pat kept staring at the card on the ceiling, while Marc scurried to clean of the mess of fallen cards for the table and floor. "So…you'll be famous for years here…and up on the ceiling."

"You're amazing," she said and kept repeating. Just then, the bell rang, and they both hurried to get to their individual classes.

That afternoon, they did share the school bus on the way to their neighborhood. Pat sat next to him, and asked Marc if he would get out at her address, so she could have a word with him. His house was only a few blocks from hers, so it wouldn't be a big trek. Besides, he was interested to know what she wanted to talk about, and didn't feel free to do so on the bus.

When the bus came to halt in front of Pat's house, the two of them exited the vehicle together. When they stood in Pat's driveway, she started by complimenting him again on the "card on the ceiling" miracle. "I'm not going to ask you how you did it…since you told me early on that the mark of a true friend is not ask a magician how he did his trick."

"That's true. Thank you," he nodded.

"But I do have something else to ask you," she said and paused.

"Anything," he answered.

After a few seconds, she waked around in a circle. Then she swallowed hard and said, "I think it would be fun if he and I went to the prom together."

Marc stood there, almost in a shocked trance and eventually responded. "Together? You and me?"

"You and me," she said again.

Marc initially reacted with a rush of emotion. At first, he could barely believe his ears. Silently, he mimed the words, "You and me." Then he involuntarily raised his hand in the air as in a victory gesture. "Yes! Yes! Yes!" he repeated and then he gave her a big hug and a sweet kiss on the cheek.

"That will be fantastic!" he added. "I'm not as good a dancer as your friend, Johnny…."

"I'd rather go with you, " she interrupted him.

"Fantastic. And by then, I will have my driver's license, so it will be perfect."

"It will make me very happy," She then gave him a return kiss on the cheek, then one on the lips, and waltzed into the house.

Pleasantly stunned, Marc followed her with his eyes as she opened the door and entered the house. He stood there for a few seconds and reminded himself that he was not in a dream. No, this was really happening.

Chapter 18

For many months, prom preparations consumed the upper class students at Hamilton High School.

Like most of her girlfriends, Pat had picked out a beautifully fluffy pastel dress. On the advice of her mother, she scheduled a hair style at the beauty parlor and a nail job weeks in advance of the actual event. Other than that, she tried to remind herself to just relax and go with the flow as the prom time approached.

Marc, on the other hand, had a few more things on his mind. One: he knew he was not a very good dancer. Admittedly, he didn't need to move like a pro, but he didn't want to embarrass Pat, who at least on stage, knew how to move. He confided this fear to his parents, who suggested that he get a few movement lessons from the local dance teacher. The woman mostly dealt with young tap dance students, but agreed to give a few private lessons to Marc, so he would feel comfortable on his feet. On his own time, in the privacy of his bedroom, he would put on some tunes and view his progress in the mirror.

The other thing was transportation to and from the event. Marc had passed his driver's test, but his family thought it would be too much of a test to go to Pat's house, then a dinner, then the Prom and then perhaps an after party. Also, they suggested that their old, dented family car was not the ideal vehicle for such an event.

His Uncle Ray came to the rescue. He suggested that as a prom gift, he would offer a limo that could transport them to all their events.

"Safer," he suggested. "More fun too," Marc answered with a thank you.

On the evening of the event, when Marc arrived at Pat's house, he was greeted by Mr. and Mrs. Foley. As usual, he was very respectful to them.

When Pat waltzed into the living room, attired in her beautiful prom dress, Marc couldn't help but remark "Wow, you look beautiful."

He also gave her a hug and presented her with a corsage, which was fortunately a good match for the dress. With Mrs. Foley's help, they attached it to the dress, and Mr. Foley brought out his camera for shots of the couple.

Pat also presented Marc with a lapel flower and pinned it to his tux. After a dozen more shots, Pat made sure she had her cellphone for more pictures and the couple walked to the limo.

The next visit was a quick bite at Lombardo's pizza parlor. As predicted, there were probably six other couples of close friends there. Everyone was super careful about not spilling tomato sauce on their elegant outfits. Even so, they were all easy and relaxed and got pics of couples, small groups, and everyone together.

Eventually, they all decided it was time to leave for the main event. Once they arrived, they entered one couple after another as if it were the Academy Awards red carpet ceremony.

Once inside, they truly did feel like celebrities. Of course, they were delighted to see all their friends so elegantly dressed. Hellos and hugs for everyone. Delicious snacks in trays. And music, music, music.

As is usually the case in most proms, it didn't lead to non-stop dancing, but it was a great background for such a special evening.

On one of the early songs ("Dancing Queen") Marc reached out for Pat's hand. Politely, he asked if he could "have this dance" with her.

Fortunately, he had actually rehearsed this one in his movement class and in front of the mirror. It had a good tempo, but was not a wild and crazy beat. As a matter of fact, it's close dance. Everytime that ABBA would sing, "You are my dancing queen," Marc would look at Pat and mouth the words. In answer to his private prayers, it was a success. Pat even complimented him on his moves and his excellent rhythm.

Between dances, they would do the rounds and gather with friends. At one point, they even ran into Johnny and Susie, who had just torn up the floor with a fast dance. Marc introduced himself to the stud and hoped he and Susie had a fun time tonight. Nice enough, but it was time for easier socializing.

Pat ran into many of her classmates and their prom dates, most of whom attended Hamilton High. After lots of greetings and compliments, the Beegees version of "You Should be Dancin'" began to play and the couple joined a group, who were all sliding back and forth. After that, they were "Dancin' in the Moonlioght." Then more snacks, and more gabfests. It all came to close after the Donna Summers recording of "Last Dance." It was perhaps Pat and Marc's most romantic moment of the evening. Like most couples, it was a slowly moving hug, culminating with an embrace and a sweet kiss on the lips.

After the event, invitees went to Carol Welton's post-prom party at her house and garden where even more pictures were snapped.

By 1:00 (as he had promised to Mr. and Mrs. Foley), he and Pat got in the limo for the final drop off at Pat's place. On the front porch, both agreed that it had been a wonderful night. There was a loving kiss generated by each and ending with a big, long lasting hug.

Marc would have liked this moment to go on for hours, but knew that all good things must come to an end. He made sure that she was safely inside, and then climbed into the limo for the last lift back to his own home.

"What a night," he whispered to himself, and hoped it would be the start of many.

Chapter 19

As idyllic as the prom was for both of them, it's impossible to be in romantic bliss forever, especially when one is only 18. After all, there are classes to attend, pajama parties to enjoy, sporting events to watch, and college admissions to consider.

Even so, Pat and Marc did spend many weekend evenings together—either watching movies or attending concerts. Pat's favorite thing was the concerts, where she could be exposed to new avenues of musical performance. Marc enjoyed them too, especially since Pat had such an affinity for songs. Often, he would ask her to sing the song to him on their walks home. A quick study, she was usually able to do so.

Movies were also a good treat, and Marc particularly enjoyed the magical escape from reality, which usually occurs in film.

Beyond that, the two just liked to hang together and imagine days to come. Not surprisingly, they would veer into slightly different paths.

Pat had always been a very bright girl, and was in fact, an honors student. This very much pleased her father, who was a college grad and professional newsman for the *New York Times*. Not surprisingly, he hoped that his daughter would follow in his footsteps.

Consequently, he encouraged her to apply to Ivy League schools throughout the United States. He preferred Harvard (his alma mater), but agreed that there were many fine universities in the Northeast and the Midwest.

Pat actually visited Yale, Princeton and NYU. She liked them all, but had a preference for NYU. Part of it was that she liked the downtown campus. Another part was the fact that she could possibly stay relatively close to Marc.

In fact, she encouraged Marc to apply to NYU with her. It was out of the question for several reasons. One: his grades were only average, and he would most likely not be accepted. Two: the son of middle class working parents, he had nothing close to the $50,000 annual tuition that would be required. Three: He wasn't even sure he was cut out for college.

In fact, it had rarely occurred to him during his time in high school. It wasn't that he was anti-college. It had just never been a burning ambition for the young man.

However, lately his friend Pat had been urging him take this step. "That way, we'll have similar experiences, and a good preparation for the future. Even if we don't end up going to the same college," she argued, "it will be a link that unites us."

If only to keep the relationship alive, Marc promised to explore that path. He looked at community colleges in the area, some state schools and public universities.

He didn't like the trade school approach. True, his father was a blue-collar worker, but Marc knew that the hours of an electrician, roofer, or carpenter were long and arduous. Deep down, he knew it would leave no time for his magic passion…and the idea of abandoning that was unacceptable to him.

If he could somehow gain some learning in business, communications or education, he could perhaps find a work/life balance that would be preferable.

Actually, Pat agreed with that ideal. While she appreciated the financial advantages of a professional life, she did not want to emulate the occupational obsession that her father embodied. He often worked 60 hours a week, especially during election times and deadline crises.

Her mother seemed to appreciate the work/life balance goal. While Mrs. Foley did work in a PR agency, she did appreciate arts and entertainment. Consequently, she was a strong supporter of Pat's enjoyment and avocation of singing and voice lessons.

Ultimately, Pat decided to sign up for NYU. She liked the fact that it offered a varied curriculum—a good mix of social science, history, and language class…along with excellent credentials in arts and letters.

After hemming and hawing for months, Marc decided to visit some of the colleges on his list. Many of them felt like extension of high school. Hunter College did not. Also, the school had scores of degree programs. He thought business studies might be interesting. He also was attracted to urban planning (which he thought might be easier) or theatre. Best of all, he liked the fact that it was maybe affordable, particularly if he got a part time job after graduating from Hamilton High. And then there was the favorable tuition factor: as part of the city college of New York system, it tuition was less than $7000 a year.

Encouraged by his ambition, his mom and dad offered to help… particularly if Marc could earn some money in the summers or as a part-time employee during the year.

As Marc saw it, there was one more advantage to Hunter College. It was in New York City, and he could possibly continue his relationship with Pat Foley. He was not at the age or stage to make long-range plans, but he did truly enjoy her friendship. At least, they could be in the same city and give it a real chance.

Mr. and Mrs. Foley had scheduled a graduation party at their home for a few dozen of Pat's friends and relatives. It was a beautiful catered event in their lovely backyard. On a presentation board, they had mounted many photos of Pat and her friends through their high school years. All of the attendees got a kick out of seeing the shared experiences. They even hired a band—not so much for dance tunes— but just as background music to add to the festivities.

Marc got there early, and as usual, was very respectful of Pat's mom and dad. In addition to his fellow classmates, who were all abuzz about the upcoming summer and future plans, he met a few of Pat's relatives, including her grandparents, who had flown in from Europe just for this event.

The snacks were excellent and after a few hours, most of the crowd thinned out. Pat asked Marc to hang in and keep her company until the end of the event. He was glad to do so, partly because it made him feel quite special.

Later that night, as Pat was reminiscing about her favorite days at Hamilton High, her grandmother presented her an envelope. "This is from your Grandpa and me, "she said. "We are so very proud of your achievements, and simply wanted to celebrate it in a significant, memorable way. Open it up," the grandma urged her.

As she did so, Pat read the beautiful sentiment…but then suddenly stopped. "Omigod. Are you kidding me?" she asked her grandparents, and rushed towards them with the note.

"Are you serious?" Pat yelped.

"We just thought that some exposure to the wider world would be a good break for you before you begin college, her grandfather said and gave her a hug.

"Two whole months in Europe?"

"Two months during the summer…all expenses paid" grandma answered. "We'll be in Ireland at the time, but you should feel free to visit other countries as well. Paris is pretty that time of year. So is Italy."

As she revealed the contents of the note, Mr. Foley had opened a bottle of champagne and poured a glass for everyone in the backyard.

"What do you think?" Pat asked Marc and showed him the note. Impressed with the generosity, he raised his hands in the air, and gave her a big hug.

"That's the trip of a lifetime. What an unbelievable gift," he responded.

As the possibilities sunk in, she compared notes with her parents who had travelled widely. "It's an amazing opportunity, " Mrs. Foley toasted her daughter and her grandparents. "I'll make sure she picks some good places and doesn't overbook her days. There is so much to see in Europe…and you don't want to rush through it."

Pat's grandmother agreed. "You could spend two months in Paris alone."

"Wow," Pat reacted all smiles.

After a sip of his champagne, Marc congratulated Pat and gave her a sweet hug. "But I should probably get on my way," he added.

"Well, I'm sure we're going to have fun together…at least in fhe first part of the summer. But then….bonjour Paris, London, Roma, Dublin…." Pat followed Marc to his car in the driveway, and gave him a kiss goodbye. She then returned to her parents and grandparents and began to fantasize about the travel adventure ahead.

Chapter 20

In June of the year, Marc and Pat had many dates together. For the most part, it was dinners where the two of them could shoot the breeze and just be comfortable with each other. They both relished their time together, especially in view of the fact that Pat would soon be gallivanting through the Old Country.

The 4th of July was spectacular. Marc popped for a Circle Line boat trip around Manhattan where they could view the fireworks from the Hudson River and the East River. It wasn't the Eiffel Tower, but it was beautiful and also very romantic. The two of them snuggled through most of the voyage and spent a good amount of time kissing each other. Both admitted they would miss holding each other, but also understood that soon they would both again be in the same city, starting new chapters in their life.

However, deep down, both knew that the days and months ahead could indeed be challenging. After all, they would be separated by an ocean—not just literally, but also psychologically. Marc instinctively believed that Pat's sense of adventure would open her to new people. Of course, he too would and should be exposed to new things. Otherwise, one lives like an old hermit.

Also, there was that inevitable reality of different paths ahead. True, they would be in the same city in the fall. However, these were different schools and very different college experiences. One was a university of the privileged or top tier high school graduates they other was a more democratic student body, and more localized population.

Also, there is that natural instinct to gain a fresh start when one takes that step into such a different stage of life. Both Pat and Marc secretly knew that it could eventually pull them apart. While it occupied their private thoughts, neither one wanted to confront it at this time.

One day at a time, Marc told himself.

Just enjoy the moment—especially the moments together, Pat similarly often reflected.

And so they did. Of course, eventually the day did come when Pat would board her plane for international destinations.

Her journey abroad began in Dublin, where she visited with her grandparents, who had a small second home there. It was a good way for her to get over jetlag and show her gratitude over several meals. Also, there were things to do in this beautiful country.

One day, her grandfather drove her to the Cliffs of Mohrer, where he explained that was where his ancestors sailed from when they immigrated to the United States. It was breathtaking.

They also took and hop-on-hop-off bus through the city of Dublin, just to get a feel for the Irish life. They then visited the Blarney

Castle, where Pat got on her back and kissed the Blarney rock for a lifetime of good luck.

Her next stop was Paris, where she booked two weeks of activities. Not surprisingly, she fell in love with this place. Her favorite site was the Eiffel Tower. It was so stunning, she could have stared at it for hours (and actually did go back to visit it a few more times).

The Champs Elysee was great for sightseeing, especially when she visited the Louvre. In New York, Pat had spent some time at the Museum of Modern Art, but had to admit the Louvre was superior both from the outside and the inside.

Staying in the swanky Hotel Moderne Saint Germain, she did meet some fellow Americans around the breakfast buffet and shared a few sights with them—Montmartre, Mont St. Michel and the Bateau Mouche boat ride on the Seine. However, her biggest thrill was the Moulin Rouge cabaret show. She loved the theatricality of the performance and of course loved the music.

Next stop: Italy. Her dad had suggested that the best sightseeing would be outside of Rome, so she only booked a few days in capital city. From there, she visited Florence, and was amazed at the art and architecture. However, her favorite Italian cities were yet to come.

To Pat, Venice was a dream. The whole idea of a city with waterways for streets was unforgettable.

Her other favorite area was the Amalfi Coast. It was a bit of a trek, but what a breathtaking site. She told herself that she could stay there for weeks, but by now, it was August, and her holiday was nearing a close. Even so, she still had one more international destination: London.

Because it bears some similarities to New York City, she instantly felt comfortable there. She often took the Metro and felt right at home. Windsor Castle made her appreciate the royalty of this historic city. The London Eye reminded her that fun is universal—wherever you find.

For culture, she took a day trip to Stonehenge and was amazed that the huge rock sculpture had existed for so many centuries.

For giggles, she would go to Covent Gardens and watch the street performers. Yes, there were many jugglers, but there were also many street magicians. As she took notes, Pat promised herself she would share these mysteries with Marc back in New York.

But one of the most memorable moments matched the experience she had watching the street singers. It reminded her how much fun it was to "sell" a song to an otherwise preoccupied audience.

Often, they would stop in their tracks. They would listen to every word. They would cry. They would laugh. Above all, they appreciated the emotion. She certainly did, and promised herself that music would always be a significant part of her life.

Eventually, all good things must come to an end. After a few more thankful calls to her grandparents and connections with her mom and dad (as she had done every week or so), she again gave her parents her flight information and spent her last night in the United Kingdom.

She thought of calling Marc a few times during her holiday and on this last evening, but believed it would only come off as a life of privilege that was truly foreign to him. Don't misunderstand, she thought of him many times, but didn't want to embarrass him or brag about her daily adventures.

Instead, she reflected on her many discoveries and packed her bags for a long journey back to NYC.

It was a nine a.m. flight that arrived before sunset at JFK. As promised, her parents had a limo waiting for her arrival and baggage pick-up.

As soon as she got home, she shared as much as she could about each country she had visited. As promised, she also texted her grandparents that she had arrived safely in NYC. And while she was at it, she thanked them once again for all she had seen and experienced.

Chapter 21

In anticipation for his college year ahead, Marc needed to get a job during the summer months to help pay his tuition. Thanks to his new friends at the Society of American Magicians, one of his compeers suggested that he apply at Tannen's Magic Shop in midtown Manhattan.

It is America's oldest magic shop, and features everything -- card tricks, books, props, close-up effects. Marc had been there a few times with his Uncle Ray and loved the place.

When he entered the shop in early July, he showed his S.A.M. membership card and told them he would be interested in working there.

Fortunately, the owner, a man named Otto Hunter, recognized him from his audition at the magic club. "I remember voting for you," Otto said. "You were good in front of all us old farts."

"Well, I tried my best," Marc understated.

The owner asked him a few more questions about his work experience (none), his particular interests in magic, and whether this was just for a summer job.

"No," Marc answered. "I'm going to Hunter College in the fall, and I could really use a part time job during the school year."

Otto the owner smiled and nodded. "I think I could use someone like you," he said. "We get a lot of professional magicians shopping in here…but we also get plenty of young kids with their parents. I think you might be able to relate to them better than someone of my age."

"I was a member of the Society of Young Magicians, before joining the bigger group, " Marc said. "I liked the kids in the group, and anyone who is interested in magic."

They discussed a few other things like schedules, pay and employment forms. After agreeing on everything, Marc and Otto shook hands and looked forward to a productive time together,

Marc started the very next day and spent most of his first few days just learning which magic tricks were in which drawers. He also got schooled in how to charge purchases for Tannen's customers. By the end of a few days, he had met most of the employees, and thoroughly enjoyed their company.

On one of those days, a father came into the store with his young 8-year old son. "We saw a magic show last week and my son loved it," the dad said. "I wonder if you could maybe suggest a few tricks to keep his early interest alive."

"Glad to," Marc said and asked the young boy's name. "Billy," he said. Marc then shook his hand. "Billy, welcome to Tannen's. My name is Marco and I know exactly how you feel. When I was your age I got hooked on magic tricks…and still am."

As he said this, Otto elbowed one of his fellow employees and winked to watch the new employee.

Marc pulled out a few easy effects. For starters, he showed him the string trick he had first performed in grade school for his friend, Pat.

"Wow, how did you do that?" Billy asked.

"Easily," Marco responded. He had checked with Otto early on about the advisability about sharing the secrets behind the effects. Otto had explained to them that he would have to use his judgment.; "If some jackass is coming into the store looking for a free show….no, you shouldn't explain how the miracle is done. However, most people who come in here want to buy a trick. They are already magicians, or future magicians. Especially if it's a young kid, you should probably explain to him that he might be quite capable of accomplishing the effect."

"We'll buy that." the dad said. "What else you got?"

Otto watched from the counter across the room with his fellow employee who was smiling and said "Marco's pretty good, He's got a knack for this."

Marc spent another half hour with the dad and his son and demonstrated four more tricks. After every one, the dad asked if his son Billy was capable of the skill.

Marc explained that he was only showing tricks that he thought the 8-year old could learn. "That's why I'm not showing any fancy card shuffles or more complicated maneuvers." Marc then suggested a few books with easy-to-learn tricks.

"I'll take them all, " the Dad said.

"And Billy, if you run into any trouble with any of these, come back and I'll explain it further and practice it with you." Marc added. "Pretty soon, you'll be doing card tricks…but one step at a time."

The dad gave Marco a credit card for the purchase. Otto entered from across the store and encouraged Marc to go through the procedure. Without a pause, he did so.

Once the customers left the store, Otto gave Marc applause. His fellow employee also gave him a thumbs up. "I think you could have a good future in this business," the owner gushed.

During those summer months, Marc worked five days a week, while Otto's other employees took their summer vacations. From Westchester County, he took the train in and out every day. He even volunteered to work every Saturday from 10-4. After all, he needed the money for college, and loved the job.

He also missed his friend Pat. He got a few texts from her in Paris and London, but didn't expect a long-distance phone conversation. Too much of a time-zone difference, and also too expensive, he told himself.

In his after hours from work, Marc tried to organize his new class schedule at Hunter College. He had decided to work a few afternoons a week at Tannen's and all day Saturday to help pay his tuition. That would enable him to take about fifteen credit hours, and still have time for homework.

He wanted a fairly easy schedule in his first semester. He decided that classes in history, music, business basics, and education were probably doable.

With his parent's and his financial contribution, he estimated he had enough for tuition. Room and board was another matter. Fact is, Hunter didn't have a plethora of dorms. However, thanks to his job at Tannen's, he did have a possible solution. One of his fellow workers—a middle-aged guy named Louie Greene, who was part of the clean-up staff—ironically needed a roommate for his mid-town apartment.

They didn't have much in common, other than the need to split finances of a small two-bedroom apartment. Marc discussed it with Louie and asked if he could see the place. It was not fancy. As a matter of fact, less than 1100 square feet. However, it was walkable to both Tannen's and Hunter College. Even more important, it was fairly affordable—only $900 each.

Marc had discussed the idea of living in NYC with his parents when he applied to Hunter. He worried that the back and forth on the train would eat up 20-25 hours a week—a bit daunting if he hoped to attend college and work part time.

Initially, his parents were not in favor. They imagined that Marc would live with them a long time---probably until he got a full-time job. The whole idea that he wanted to attend college was something of a surprise to them, but they were completely supportive of the fact that he wanted to achieve more in life.

They also appreciated the fact that he had summer job and part-time income during the school year. Consequently, they agreed to split the expenses and proudly wish him well.

In assessing the new small apartment, Marc decided he only needed bedroom furniture, clothing and luggage for his magic tricks. Thanks to his parents, they agreed to help him move these items into the city a few days before his college debut.

The parents were privately very saddened by Marc's impending departure. However, they also congratulated themselves on being successful parents who had raised a son with ambition. "After all, isn't that the goal?" his dad said one late night. Reluctantly, his mom agreed. Fortunately, Marc would come to visit them many times in the next few years.

Chapter 22

Pat had returned from Europe jet-lagged, but excited about getting things in order for the year ahead.

She called Marc first thing in the morning to touch base with him and tell him that she had missed him. In the conversations, she discovered that he registered at Hunter College, and had landed a job at Tannen's.

"Geez, that sounds exciting," she remarked.

"It's a great job. Lots of fun and fairly manageable hours. I'll even be able to work there a few times a week during the school year. Oh, and one more thing: I even found an apartment in the city for during the school year.

It's small, but convenient to both Hunter and my job."

"Wow, you have been busy," she complimented him. "I have so much to do in the next few weeks before NYU starts. Give me a few days, but then I want to get together with you and have a few laughs."

"I definitely want to do that. Can't wait," he told her, and they scheduled a dinner for the weekend.

In the next few days, Pat made sure that she was registered for all her upcoming classes. She had decided to take a basic journalism class in honor of her father…but also classes in political science, psychology, and of course, music.

The bigger task ahead was securing her dorm. Her parents had paid a deposit at the beginning of summer, but she was required to view the proposed room and sign a form.

Most of the rooms had been already assigned, but there were still a few that were available. They were all 2BR layouts with 2 bathrooms. None were big. But Brittany Hall did have a rec room, music room, a study lounge, and a laundry room.

As part of the registration, the university offered a service that tried to match incoming freshmen with possible room mates who had similar interests.

Pat had filled out a form before her trip to Europe, but by now most of Her interested candidates had found a roommate. Even so, she was able to peruse a few other late applicants and even talk to them by phone. After several calls, she did have a conversation with Anna Miller who had applied late. She was from St. Louis, Missouri and was interested in studying musical theatre. She had been in two high school musicals and believed New York City was the place to be.

Pat immediately thought Anna would be a good roommate. At least, they would similar interests on TV shows and maybe even off

Broadway plays. They compared notes about move-in dates and both agreed that it could be a good pairing.

In view of the fact that she had her ducks in the row for her upcoming first semester at NYU, Pat called Marc to fill him in and try to schedule as many get-togethers as possible in the upcoming weeks.

Their first date was on that Friday night. Both tried their best to explain how they spent their summer…and show interest in the other person's progress.

Quite honestly, Marc was envious of all her trips and discoveries abroad. He particularly liked the fact that she had brought him back a list of favorite tricks she had seen the street magicians perform in London. "So you were thinking of me?" he exclaimed.

"I thought of you often on the trip," she reassured him, "but I didn't want to bug you from afar. I figured you might have your hands full during the summer months."

"I did," he admitted. "But I missed you tons." To dramatize the point, he atypically got up from the dinner table and kissed her. "I am so happy you are back in town and we have a little time before our classes start."

That night, they closed out the evening with a walk along the Hudson River under the moonlight. Along the way, there were plenty of hugs and passionate kisses.

The next few weeks were just as emotional for them. They went to a few free concerts in the park, and had a few double dates with their buddies or girlfriends as the summer was coming to a close. Everyone at that age was busy, busy, busy, getting their lives in order for the next stage. Most of them knew that the various colleges would inevitable pull them apart, especially if their chosen schools were in different states. Consequently, they all tried to savor every minute together.

Even so, Pat and Marc probably had their best times just together with each other. They often went to a museum or botanical garden on the weekend, and frequently had romantic dinners with each other. Obviously, they each had important times with their parents in the closing days of the summer before college started.

Marc's mom and dad were rather sad that their dear boy would be moving into an apartment. However, they were proud of his maturity in progressing to the next stage. They also enjoyed seeing Pat when he was with her, and were very supportive of that relationship. Every once in a while, they would have a barbecue in the back yard, and enjoy the chemistry between the young couple.

On one of those barbecues, Uncle Ray joined the immediate family. He brought good tidings from his friends at Tannen's, who bragged about the Job Marco was doing sharing tricks with the young customers. "Otto says you are one of the best hires he has ever made," Ray told his favorite nephew. "And I hear you are going to work there part-time throughout the school year!" he gleefully exclaimed.

After a weekend of fun together, there were only a few days before each of them had to check into their new city residences. In those remaining days, they simply enjoyed quiet romance. Privately, they both hoped that in their new paths ahead, there would still be plenty of time for future romance.

Chapter 23

Marc enjoyed most of his new classes at Hunter. His favorites so far were business basics, and music. The business basics class was relevant to job at Tannen's. If he hit a snag in class, he would ask his boss Otto about how it worked in the real world.

His interest in these topics just impressed his boss all the more. Examples: How do you know how much to order for the holiday season? How do you deal with customers who are habitually slow to pay their bills? How can you handle advertising and publicity? How do you keep the working attitude fresh?

"By hiring people like you," Otto told Marc. "You've rejuvenated a lot of us be more engaging with our customers—especially the young ones."

Marc blushed at compliment, but did honestly enjoy the give and take with young customers. In a way, they helped him stay practiced with new tricks. Inevitably, They also improved his presentation skills. After all, you can't just demo an effect. You have to "sell" the impact.

Marc also got a kick out his music class. Thankfully, it wasn't all classical overtures. The teacher was smart enough to know that 18-19 year olds like current music—so he did a good job mixing it with trends of the more modern decades. Marc couldn't help but reflect on Pat when he heard the more contemporary songs. Hearing the melodies, he was often reminded of what a good voice she had.

Sometimes, he would call her after a class and share a few song from Linda Ronstadt ("I've Got a Crush On You"), Dinah Washington ("Cry Me a River") Dionne Warwick ("That's What Friends Are For") and many others. Pat was familiar with most of the songs, primarily from her voice teacher, Michelle.

Even so, she appreciated the tips and enjoyed reconnecting with Marco.

They would get together a couple times a week—usually one school night a week for a quick dinner. Usually, on Sunday for an afternoon in the city. One of their favorite things was renting one of those citi bikes and pedaling up the path along the Hudson. It was a beautiful view and good exercise from sitting in class all week.

Unlike Marc, Pat's classes were more difficult. Poly Sci required a lot of reading. Her journalism class called for writing at least one news story a week. She would ordinarily scour the *New York Times* for local headlines in the news. It usually took several phone calls to solicit some quotes. Often, it necessitated background research in the library. As one could predict, she thoroughly enjoyed her music class, but it was largely instrumental classical overtures.

To compensate, her roommate Anna kept Pat up to speed on current tunes. Consequently, they often listened to Elton John, Michael Buble, Rihanna, Ariana Grande, and Ed Sheeran. Irresistable, they would sometimes quietly sing along with the tracks. Often, they would listen to soundtracks of musicals and secretly wish they could be in one—if only they had the time or a gap in the crowded schedule.

One afternoon, Anna came into her dorm room carrying a flyer from music class. She was all excited. It was an audition call for a musical called "The Fantasticks." The good news: it was open only to underclassmen and required only three weeks of rehearsals. Unlike the more elaborate productions, this one only had seven cast members, and was always produced on a stage with minimal set pieces—usually a bench, a few stools and a few props.

"Should we give it a shot?" Pat asked.

"When is the show?" Anna asked and looked again at the flyer for the fine print. "Oh, no….the show is right after Christmas break. So they will want to rehearse during the 2 week holiday hiatus. I can't do that..I promised my mom and dad I would visit them and the rest of the family during those weeks in St. Louis."

"Maybe they could come here to New York instead of the other way around." Pat offered.

"No, I've got a big family in the Midwest, and I already made them a promise I would be there." Anna explained. "But you should definitely audition," she told Pat. "It won't even get in the way of your class schedule."

"I'll think about it," Pat answered, and decided to preview the songs and look on the computer to familiarize herself with some of the scenes.

At the audition in early November, Pat decided to use the same songs she had learned for "Grease." True, this was a very different kind of musical, but "Hopeless Devoted to You" was the same sort of ballad that was rather typical of "The Fantasticks." Also, she knew the song well…having sung it dozens of times just a few years ago.

A week later, she learned that she had been cast in the role of Louisa. There would be only three rehearsals before the holiday break—just to learn the songs and deal with limited blocking.

She immediately called her parents and told them the good news—also that she would most likely be occupied throughout most of the Christmas break. They were disappointed they would not be able to see her more during that period, but sincerely congratulated her.

She then called Marc, who was delighted to hear that she would again be utilizing her god-given talent. He didn't know anything about the musical, but quite honestly was rarely disappointed with any of them. As for her rehearsals during the Christmas break, he assured her that he would most likely be in the city those days. He assumed that Tannen's would want to increase his hours during the break to give their other workers off for more family shopping. At least, he hoped so…. since he could use the money for the next semester.

Pat truly enjoyed the musical rehearsals. It's a sweet story with easy, hummable songs. The most famous one is "Try to Remember," which is sung by the narrator of the play, a character named El Gallo.

The role of Luisa is a young woman who has a thing for a character named Matt. Unlike the romantic entanglement she experienced in "Grease," she had no true heartthrob for Matt. He was a nice enough guy, but not a boyfriend of her dreams. (If she wanted romance, she had Marc down the street).

She loved singing "Soon It's Gonna Rain," "They Were You," and "Love, You Are Love." She also loved the fact that the musical had no raucous dance numbers like "Grease." It was mostly just boy-girl duets, occasionally presented with easy strolling on stage. Perhaps that's why it had such an abbreviated rehearsal schedule.

Her biggest thrill of the holiday run-throughs was the extra-curricular evenings after. By the time the rehearsal were in full swing, Pat's roommate Anna had vacated the dorm for a promised visit with her family in St. Louis. Many of the other dorm residents had also used the weeks to visit with their parents. As a result, the Brittany Hall residence Hall was very deserted and lonely.

Fortunately, Marc's hotel residence was not. Marc's roommate Billy normally worked nights, but at this time of year, he had decided to take a week or two off to get some sunshine in Florida. As a result, Marc and Pat spent many late nights together.

Until this time, they had never had sex. Yes, they had hugged and passionately kissed, but had always demurred consummating the relationship in the seat of a car. Somehow, it just seemed cheap to both of them.

Marc's small apartment was not elegant, but it did have a full sized bed, a TV and fridge. After Christmas break rehearsals, Pat would usually catch a cab to his mid-town apartment.

Fairly exhausted from a three-hour rehearsal, she would usually have a glass of wine with Marc just to unwind. Often, they would then compare notes of their days, and sometimes just turn on the TV to catch the latest news. Be then, they would toast each other and get more comfortable under the covers.

Neither one was a wild sex freak. They were not screamers. They were not fans of porno videos. Instead, they both enjoyed a more romantic, personal liaison of gentle touching and long embraces. Yes, they would culminate this foreplay with true physical sex—sometimes more than once. But when they had satisfied each other, they each enjoyed the quiet time together with smiles on their faces.

All this started to become beautifully contagious for both Pat and Marc. At least during the Christmas break, they would enjoy each other's company 4-5 times a week. On their Sundays, they would both visit their parents in Westchester, but then renew their nights together until their schools started again. What fun!

By the first week of January, each of their roommates were back, and Pat's rehearsals were in their final week for a January 4-6 opening weekend. Not surprisingly, these were longer rehearsals...especially given the generous schedule that preceded. Consequently, Pat and

Marc's conversations were mostly by phone for several early January days. Nice, but not quite the same as those sweet nights together.

Pat reflected on those evenings together in setting the mood for her songs. As usual, it helped make each of her musical songs more emotionally convincing.

On her opening weekend, Marc promised to be there every night. On the first weekend, he met Pat's roommate Anna, who admitted she had heard about him and was happy that he could keep Pat company while she was in the Midwest. During the performance, both were impressed with the production, and particularly Pat's rendition of the songs. As a nice guy, Marc understood that they both might enjoy a night together and excused himself from this roommate get-together.

The next night, Mr. and Mrs. Foley attended. When Marc saw them enter, he rushed up to them and told them he was so glad to see them again. Sitting next to them, they all agreed it was a wonderful, stirring production, starring Pat Foley. Afterwards, he gave them all a hug and correctly assumed they would like to have dinner alone with their daughter.

On the closing afternoon production, it was a smaller crowd and Marc sat by himself in the audience. It gave him a chance to view the true flow of the show, and focus primarily on the performance of Pat.

He was again bowled over.

There was a short cast party after the show, and Pat invited Marc. He graciously congratulated each of the cast members on their performances. Pat was very happy with the show, and her role in it.

She was even happier with her evening in Marc's apartment. It was nice to feel so embraced and appreciated by one who knew what it takes to impress an audience.

Chapter 24

Marc enjoyed his part-time job at Tannen's Magic Shop. It gave him an opportunity to meet many local magicians. It helped give him a grounding in business for his college classes on that subject. It also automatically made him a better magician. Part of it was the exposure to so many new tricks. Part of it was that he often had to demonstrate the method once he sold something to a customer.

One side benefit was the magic shows every Wednesday and Thursday night at 8 p.m. It was normally performed by Owen Levine and is called Magic After Hours. It was basically a close-up show with perhaps a dozen people around one table and one spotlight overhead. Marc went to the show occasionally, but usually had to get home and do some homework for his college classes at Hunter.

On the Monday of the week, his boss Otto asked Marc if he could fill in for Owen on Wednesday for about a half-hour. "Owen is going to be out town that evening…and I hate to disappoint the folks who come here for a show. I've seen you demonstrate tricks. You're good. And I think you might enjoy it," his boss told Marc. "I'll do the last half-hour, but if you could do two or three tricks up front, I think the audience might enjoy it," Otto said.

"A half-hour?" Marc asked. "I think I could handle that."

"Good," his boss answered. "You should just stay after work on Wednesday and set up everything because the show starts at 8.p.m."

"I look forward to it," Marc answered and went back to his apartment to practice a routine. He also called Pat, explained the new one-night gig, and invited her to attend.

"That sounds like fun," she exclaimed. "I will definitely be there. Afterwards, you want to get a bite together?"

"I want to spend the whole night with you," he responded. "My roommate Billy will again be out of town, so we could have a little fun after the show. I'll set an alarm so you can get up early and make your classes…and so I can make mine, too."

"Indeed, that does sound like a fun night," she answered and promised to attend.

On Wednesday evening, he greeted beforehand and made sure she had a good seat in front.

"Are you all set?" she asked.

"Hope so. I've practiced the last few nights."

"You'll be great," she said and gave him a hug.

By 8 p.m., the crowd had assembled in the Tannen's showroom. Once they were seated, Otto took the stage and welcomed them. "Thank you all for coming to 'Magic After Hours." As many of you know, this is usually hosted by Owen Levine…but he is caught in a flight from the West Coast (yes, a slight fib). Hey, but don't you worry. We have a good show for you right here…tonight. To get things going, I'd like to introduce you to one of my favorite magicians. His name is Marco the Magnificent.

"For some of you who visit the shop as customers, you already probably already know Marco. He works with me behind the counter and helps instill the magic arts for many of our younger customers. He's the youngest member of the Society of American Magicians in New York, and a great guy. Please….a nice round of applause for Marco the Magnificent."

With that, Marc took the stage and waved to the crowd. "Thank you. I am so happy to be here tonight, and want you all to relax and have a good time. I am not going to release any wild animals out of cage or cut you in half just for the sake of applause. No, this is mostly close-up stuff…so pull your chairs around the table and be amazed."

With that, most people gathered their chairs around the semi-circle table. As there were eleven people, it was about two deep. My first effect is a thing called "Miser's Dream"….since it's a way that a magician can make money out of thin air."

He then pointed to the youngest member of the audience. "What's your name, young man?" he asked.

The kid answered that his name was Jeffrey and that he was eight years old. Marc asked him to join him up front and asked "Jeffrey, you got any money on you?" The magician looked at the audience and said, "See, this is how magicians get rich." There were some chuckles. Then Marc grabbed a metal bucket and showed the audience that it was empty.

He then said, "Watch!" and reached his right hand towards young Jeffrey's right ear. He pantomimed tossing the coin in the air. With his left hand, he grabbed the metal pail and watched the imaginary coin fly through the air…and then go "Clang" inside the bucket.

"How'd you do that?" Marc asked the young kid, who smiled and shrugged.

Marco then reached towards the young kid's right elbow for an imaginary coin. Once again, it went "Clang" inside the bucket.

Then he reached under Jeffrey's chin. Another clang.

Then under Jeffrey's left elbow. Another clang. And another. And another. And another.

Then Marco pointed in space and "caught" another imaginary coin. And another clang. And another.

Finally, he pointed to the young kid's eyes and again invited the audience to watch. He then watched the journey of coin in the air and walked across the stage with his metal can and "caught" the coin in mid air.

For a conclusion, he turned the bucket over and poured out about a dozen coins.

"How about a nice round of applause for my rich friend Jeffrey? Jeffrey, here's a momento for you," Marco then gave the young boy a half dollar souvenir for his participation.

There were generous hand-claps from everyone in the audience.

Marco then reached towards the counter and brought out some props for his next trick.

On the table in front of him, he presented the proposition. "Three cups. Three balls." He showed each cup to be empty and then placed three small balls on top of each one.

One by one, with several slight-of-hand moves, the balls seemed to disappear into thin air….and then reappear under each of the cups.

But wait, there's more! The big climax is yet to come. He shows the inside of each cup to be empty and then lifts each one to reveal three larger surprises. Instead of three small balls, each lifted cup now reveals a fresh orange. In fact, when he reaches and again lifts the middle cup, a fourth orange magically appears. As he hears the applause, he gives the first three oranges to members of the audience who have greatly enjoyed the illusion.

Marco smiles and then looks at his watch. "I think I have time for one more miracle." He then reaches in his coat pocket and takes out a fresh deck of cards. "Who likes card tricks?" he teases the audience. They all raise their hands.

"Would you help me with this one," he asks and points to a young lady In the front row. "What is your name?"

"I am Cheryl," the attractive young woman answers.

"Cheryl, I want you to look at this deck of cards," he said as he fanned the deck. "As you can see, they are all different." He then held the deck in his right hand and dropped 8-10 cards at a time into his left. "Tell me when to stop."

She did and he asked her to memorize the next card. "Don't tell me what it is. In fact, show it to the other people in the audience so they too will know the suit and value—whether it's a face card or a picture card."

"Now I want you to do something destructive. I want you to tear off the left top corner of that card. To demonstrate, let me show you the size of the ripped corner you should aim for. For example, if your card is the king of hearts, you would tear off the K and the heart. If your card were the three of clubs, you'd tear off the three and the club. Watch me. He then took out a joker and showed her the ideal size, as he tore off the upper left about a half inch in each direction.

"OK, give me the card and corner. You're not going to forget your card are you? "

She shook her head no.

"Just to make sure, hold on the corner so no one can forget it." He then gave her the card corner and took the remainder of the card and put it in the deck. He then shuffled, and put the deck down to his left.

Immediately, Marc reached in his jacket pocket and took out a small magic wand. "Time for some real magic," he declared. "Cheryl, I am going to turn over the deck and show all the faces of the cards. Take a look and tell me if you see your card.

Cheryl looked and looked but could not find the card.

"That's strange. Maybe I need something more than a magic wand," he teased. He then reached in his jacket pocket and brought out a kitchen knife. "It's a magic knife," he declared.

He reached for the last remaining orange on the table and looked underneath it. "Is your card hiding underneath? No, maybe it's inside." Then with a flourish he used his knife to cut the fresh orange in half.

Inside, there was a rolled up card. As he took it out of the orange, he said, "For the first time, Cheryl what was your card?"

She answered "the eight of spades."

Marco then unfurled the orange-soaked card and presented it to the audience. "The eight of spades…almost." he said. "It's just missing a top left corner. Cheryl. Let's see if that corner in your hand fits."

"Miraculously, it does (otherwise, it wouldn't be a magic trick)." The crowd gave him a large round of applause. He gratefully bowed and introduced his boss, Otto.

Otto took the stage and the applause continued. "I thought you might like Marco the Magnificent," he boasted. "OK, a tough act to follow, but I'll do my best."

The owner of the place had clearly done many shows. He often giggled with the audience and seemed to have as much fun showing a new trick as the crowd had in seeing it. He showed affects using silks, ropes, and dice. After his half hour, he bowed and thanked the audience for attending.

Many of them milled around in the store, and shook hands with Otto and with Marc. When they started to clear, the young magician introduced Pat to the owner of Tannen's.

"Nice to meet you. Great job," she said shaking his hands. "And you—Mr. Marco the Magnificent—you had a great show. You've improved a lot since you started working here."

"Nahh, he started good, from the moment he walked through the door," Otto gushed. "And now you're off duty, Marco. Go have some fun."

"We will try to," Marc responded.

"Try? We're gonna have a lot of fun," Pat said with a wink. As she did so, the two of them walked out of the shop and kissed all the way down the elevator ride. When they reached the ground floor, they walked the eight blocks to Marc's vacant apartment.

It was a grand night. Lots of smiles. Lots of fun. Lots of sex.

Chapter 25

The early summer months flew by.

Marc had decided to take a break from his school workload, and work full-time at Tannen's. He thoroughly enjoyed it and appreciated the extra cash that the job afforded. He even found the time to do a few of those evening magic shows, which were an added thrill.

By contrast, Pat decided to take NYU classes during the summer. It required a fair amount of homework, but even so, it did allow her enough time explore some off-Broadway plays and musicals with her roommate, other classmates, and with Marc.

The two of them always tried to have dinner together at least once or twice a week. On one of those evenings, Pat did share her surprising plans for the upcoming year. She announced that she had been accepted to NYU's semester abroad program in London.

"London?" he asked incredulously. "You're going to go to school in London?"

"It's a great opportunity," she answered with some genuine excitement in her voice. "They accept about 500 students from NYU each semester, and offer more than 80 courses."

"Wow, you're going to be gone a whole semester?" he responded with a definite tinge of sadness.

"My dad recommended it, and they're footing the entire bill. They're even planning to visit me during Thanksgiving."

"That's great," Marc said, trying to fake some enthusiasm.

"The best thing about it," she explained, "is that many of the classes include field work and site visits….so I get to not only study, but get to explore more of the U.K."

"You're a very luck girl," he nodded.

After a few minutes, she reached out and took Marc's hand. "Why don't you come and visit me?"

He just slowly shook his head no. "I've got to work during that semester…and I have Hunter college in the city here. Fact is, I don't really have the money to do that. But I will miss you…a lot more than you could ever imagine."

"I will miss you, too," she quickly added. "But we have all summer to have kicks. Maybe we should start tonight."

After splitting the bill, they walked slowly hand-in-hand to Marc's apartment. After listening to some music on the stereo, they jumped into bed and had an evening of sex together. Somehow, Marc felt it was less than 100% romance. The whole idea that he would have a complete semester without her weighed on him.

Of course, they still had many months together, but in his heart, he know she would be off to Europe before long.

In the remaining summer months, the two of them did their best to enjoy each other's company as much as possible.

One Sunday, they went to the South Street Seaport and visited all the shops and boats. On a different Sunday afternoon, they toured Brooklyn Heights and Prospect Park, which is actually bigger than Central Park. Of course, they also went to free concerts along the Hudson River and enjoyed picnics with some of their Westchester friends. One of those concerts featured award-winning music, which particularly pleased the couple. Marc knew most of the melodies. Pat knew most of the words, and she would sing to him in the car as he would drive her back to her parent's home in Dobbs Ferry, New York.

Despite this whirlwind of summer fun, both knew that the days were numbered. Soon, by the end of August, Pat would need to pack her bags, and Marc would need to prepare for another year of study and magic in New York City.

One long weekend, they actually went to Long Beach Island—one of the best beach resorts near NYC. Here, they were able to take a fishing boat ride, enjoy easy lunches together, and walk along the beautiful shore.

On their last night together, Marc and Pat did their best to ignore tomorrow and shared a night of music at a club in lower Manhattan.

The featured performer sang many of the hits of contemporary artists—Celine Dion, Lady Gaga, Katy Perry, and Adele.

"She's good," Pat couldn't help but remark.

"Not as good as you," Marc winked at her and held her hand. She just sighed, and smiled at him. "You know, you have been an amazing magical friend ever since grade school," she struggled and started to say, but then felt a tear roll down her cheek.

"Don't cry," Marc said and took a napkin to wipe away her tear. "You're going to have an amazing time in London."

After a few seconds of silence, he then added, "Look me up when you get back."

"Of course, I will," she said, hugged him, and at least at the time, truly meant it. But both instinctively knew that it would be a challenging period ahead.

Chapter 26

Pat's parents brought her to JFK airport the next day for a noon flight to London.

During breakfast, mom and dad made sure she had the credit cards she needed and enough money in her Chase Bank Account to deal with any U.K. needs. Not surprisingly there were plenty of hugs and kisses. Once inside the terminal, they made sure that their dear daughter had all the tickets, school info, and reading matter she needed for the upcoming flight.

When she had passed check-in and immigration, she proceeded to her gate, and saw many other young people her own age. She couldn't help but think that many of them might be headed to NYU London. Could be. But rather than ask in the terminal, she correctly figured she would meet her new classmates soon enough.

At her window seat, she couldn't help but look though the glass at the NYC skyline, and think that she might miss it, particularly her time with Marc. However, she reminded herself that a bright new season was just over the horizon, and could perhaps be life-changing.

In preparation, she looked at her upcoming classes at NYU-London. In view of the change of continents, she did her best to make sure that her courses would hold her interest. She had signed up for International Relations, Art and Architecture, Literature and Theatre, and (at the request of her father) a journalism course.

Once she landed safely at Heathrow, she took a black cab to her residence hall in Central London. It was called the Guilford House and it was a beautiful old building with a white stone front. The rooms were small, but it did have a lounge on the first floor and it was within easy walking distance of the campus. Like most of the residence halls, it did not have kitchen facilities, but there were plenty of small cafes in the neighborhood for breakfast, lunch and dinner.

After making a call to let her parents know she had arrived safely, she went to the lounge and met several students. Rosa Jackson and Linda Crosby were both from the New York area (Brooklyn and Ft. Lee, New Jersey). Daniel Taylor was from Virginia Beach. All of them had just completed their freshman year at NYU. All of them were also hungry and walked together to the nearby Willis Café.

Most offered similar reasons for taking a semester abroad—adventure, exposure to a wider world, and the fun of exploration. Daniel had a slightly more academic reason. He liked art and architecture and thought London specifically could expand his horizons. Pat mentioned that she was taking that class in London, and that she had a few other interests, writing and theatre. They all agreed that theatre in London was rumored to rival Broadway.

After dinner, they all returned to the Guilford House and individually prepared for their first big day at NYU London.

Pat's first class was international relations, where she saw Rosa again a few rows to her right. They were both happy to share the same class and agreed that they could compare notes and discuss the day's lessons if anything was confusing.

Pat's next class was journalism, which promised to be challenging. The professor told them that they would all have a written assignment due every two weeks, on a subject of his choice. The first topic? An opinion piece: What is the true appeal of Madame Tussaud's? It would require a visit to the wax museum, but Pat truly believed that would be enjoyable.

Her last class of the day was Art and Architecture. When she entered the classroom, she saw Daniel Taylor already seated. He motioned to Pat to come join him in the desk just to his left.

The teacher, a British architect named Dr. Richard Slater, explained that he had purposely scheduled this class later in the day because he wanted to combine it with field trips. "Why study art and architecture with photos?" he asked. "Isn't it better to see the real thing…especially in a city like London that is replete with amazing art and architecture."

As soon as he said so, Daniel looked across at Pat gestured a "thumbs up."

"We'll go to the London Dungeon, the British Museum, Windsor Castle, Covent Gardens, Hyde Park…and a bunch of other sites. Are you all cool with that? It might require an extra hour of class time…but I believe it will imminently be worth it. Please raise your hand if that gets in the way of your schedule. "

No student did. As a result, the professor explained that class participation was key, and there would be only two term papers. He also gave a syllabus of all the sites they would be studying. It truly did look like fun.

When the class ended, Daniel asked if he could buy Pat a cocktail.

"Yes, of course," she answered. "That would be nice." The two of them discussed the promise of the class and agreed that it might be their favorite of the curricula.

Daniel was a handsome man with some Southern charm. After some conversation about their first class together, he told her that he might be interested in eventually becoming an architect, but admitted that it was a long way off. "And what about you?" he asked.

"I don't know. I like journalism, but secretly, I like music and love to sing. Of course, my folks are not so thrilled about that artistic pursuit. But I like it. I just don't know if that's any way to ever make a living."

"Who cares? If it's a passion, and you're good at it…there might be a way."

"I like the way you think," she answered.

After the glasses of wine, they walked back to the residence hall, and said goodnight. Pat truly had enjoyed the evening—perhaps because it was the only time of the day when she was not "trying to fit in" in a foreign land.

It was an easy tete-a-tete. Given the proposed schedule of site visits, she believed there would be many more such evenings.

Chapter 27

Pat enjoyed her early weeks at NYU London, and did her best to balance classwork with sightseeing. She enjoyed the Jack the Ripper tour, the changing of the guard, and Madame Tussaud's Wax Museum (She opined that the chance to stand next to famous figures inevitable spiked one's interest in their true lives, history, and achievements. Much more effective than reading about them in a book).

She also relished her Art and Architecture visits to Tate Museum, the National History museum, and the Tower Bridge. After each of these instructional visits, she shared a glass of wine with her new friend, Daniel Taylor. It gave each of them a chance to reflect on the class lessons, and get to know each other better.

Without being pushy, Pat couldn't help but feel that Daniel was interested in her. He would often ask about her interest in music, and did want to explore a few London musicals with her. They viewed "Mama Mia" together and enjoyed a few of the songs ("Dancin' Queen," and "Mama Mia, Here We Go Again"). For a taste of nostalgia, they also enjoyed "Carousel" and those famous songs by Rogers and Hammerstein—'If I Loved You," and "June is Bustin' Out All Over.")

She did feel some attraction to Daniel, but didn't want to repeat the tryst that she had with Johnny, her co-star from "Grease," Fortunately, Daniel was not that kind of sex freak. He was more of a gentle soul, like Marco. However, he was here in London and Marc was thousands of miles away.

Rather than fall off a cliff together, Pat decided to take is slowly. One day at a time.

In the ensuing weeks, she decided to enjoy her days in London. There was plenty of homework to keep her busy, and of course, more attractions in the U.K.'s biggest city. Also, she reminded herself that it would not be long before her parents would visit her at Thanksgiving time.

When they arrived, Mr. and Mrs. Foley simply wanted to visit with their dear daughter. There was no need to sightsee or take jump-on, jump-off bus tours.

They stayed at the Mayfair Hotel, a 5 star property in a beautiful neighborhood. Every day of the weekend, they spent the afternoon together with long walks in Hyde Park and delicious dinners in London's best restaurants.

Not surprisingly, they were mostly interested in her well-being and adjustment to this capital city.

"Do you like it better than New York?" her dad asked. "If so, maybe you could spend a whole year here."

"I love it," she answered with a smile. "But I do miss New York City, and will want to come back after the semester."

"Are you enjoying your journalism classes," Dad asked, since that was a priority of his.

"It's a great course," she admitted. "But all my classes are great."

"Have you made new friends here?" her mom innocently asked.

"Yes, many are from NYU back home. One guy in particular has been very nice to me here. Occasionally, we go to dinner or a play together."

"Oh, good," dad encouraged. "I was hoping you might meet a good guy. Is he British?"

"No….dad, he's from NYU," she corrected him. "And it's not that kind of relationship. Just a friend. He's a nice guy…like Marc."

Mr. Foley just raised his eyebrows. It's not that he didn't like Marco. Actually, he did… given the courtesy and manners that he always showed to him and his wife. He just thought that his daughter was a spectacular soul, and he wanted a superstar for her.

They had never discussed her relationships with guys. Somehow, dad just instinctively knew that that topic was verboten with a smart, sensitive daughter.

Pat's mother changed the subject. She explained that Pat's grandparents wanted to visit her, but that this weekend was bad for them, since they were out of the country. Pat reiterated that she was so thankful that they had first exposed her to Europe after their generous high school graduation gift.

In the remaining hours and days, Pat and her parents discussed life in Westchester County. She had plenty of questions about her neighborhood friends and was happy to know that her parents were still plugged in on their progress.

After the Thanksgiving weekend, her parents did give all good wishes and warm hugs…and promised to look forward to her return around Christmas time.

"Hopefully, you'll be able to spend some time with us rather than in your dorm."

"Definitely, " she promised. The young woman did indeed look forward to that holiday, and all it would hold for her.

Of course, she still had weeks of classes to attend in London, and some enjoyable get-togethers with her friend, Daniel.

That particular relationship was a bit of a puzzle for Pat. He was a very attractive man, and always seems delighted to be with her. Often, she would reflect on how happy she was to have made his acquaintance in this foreign country. Sometimes, she wondered how she would react if he made a play for sexual intimacy.

One night, about a week before their planned return to the U.S,, he did address the issue. "My god, you have been a fantastic companion all semester," he began. "And you are a sexy young woman as well."

Ah, here it comes, she thought. Danny boy has been saving his best lines for the last act.

They clincked glasses. He took a sip of his wine and toasted her. "Pat, my dear, here's to you." He then continued. "Ever wonder why we never wound up in bed together? "

She took a sip and nodded to him. "Well, the question and the thought has occurred to me too."

"I feel I owe you an explanation," he explained. "I think you are the most beautiful, attractive, and interesting person I have met since being in London. But here's the rug-pull: I have a deep commitment to woman in Virginia Beach, and I'm not the kind of guy to screw around.

"Quite frankly, I don't think of you as a 'screw around' girl. No, you are a wonderful soul…and if the situation was different, you would be my deep commitment, and we would spend time having sweet sex, but I am, deep down, a faithful guy." He then took a pause. "Hope you understand."

Pat was smiling and reached across to touch his hand. "Daniel, quite simply, I admire you even more than I did ten minutes ago. You are an amazing guy, and if the circumstances were different, who the hell knows what might have happened between us."

She paused. "And how's this for irony? We are in the same boat. I too have a loved one back home, and it was a big worry that I would be somehow tempted to cheat on him. And yes, dear Daniel, just so you know, I was tempted, just being with you."

"But you are a true-blue champ. Maybe that's why I have been so drawn to you from the start," she added.

Daniel smiled, stood up and gave her the most affectionate kiss on the lips. "Wow, I hope our missing partners know how absolutely great we both are."

"I'll bet they do," Pat replied. "I hope we can still go out together until we return back home to our dear loves."

"I hope we can go out every evening," he concluded.

They did just that. These were no-pressure dates, and were filled with spontaneous fun. Both were very proud of their faithfulness, and completely delighted to go out with a kindred spirit.

Chapter 28

There was much about Pat's trip to the U.K. that she truly enjoyed. However, it did feel good to be back in New York in plenty of time to prepare for Christmas and reconnect with Marc.

In fact, she had called him from her London dorm before she left. It was a sincere call that alerted him to her schedule, U.S. arrival and her first day of the new semester. And oh yes, it communicated one more important thing. "I missed You, Marc" " she told him. "I hope we can get together before the semester starts."

"You bet," he happily responded. "I'm dying to see you."

"Me, too," she agreed. "Of course, I will need to spend some time with my mom and dad just to get all my clothes clean and overcome the jet lag. But I'll give you a call soon and I definitely want to get together."

"A kiss and a hug from New York," he said and concluded the call.

Upon reflection, Marc had to admit it was an unusual call. True, they had agreed upfront to not waste money on day-to-day doings an Atlantic Ocean apart. However, in their time together, she had rarely seemed so very anxious to spend time with each other.

Marc invited her to the Union Square Café in midtown towards the end of the week. Since his Tannen's work schedule normally ended at 6 p.m., he safely scheduled it for 7:30 just in case there were some late customers.

He got there early and staked out a good table with a view. When Pat arrived, she immediately saw him and skipped across the floor to give him a big hug.

"Marco the Magnificent," she exclaimed.

"Pat the Pretty One," he countered.

She giggled and asked him if he had rehearsed that line.

"Not really," he responded. "It just occurred to me when I saw you after all these months. "A Feast for the Eyes," he added.

"Wow, you've gotten smooth since I've been out-of-town." Pat countered with a sweet wink.

Like a gentleman, he put her winter coat on the empty chair and then sat next to her. Their conversation was a rat-a-tat of details on both of their parts. Marc explained that he done well in school and had thoroughly enjoyed his gig at Tannen's. He was proud to report that he had a few after-hours shows at the magic store, and learned quite a few new tricks.

"Have you seen any new plays or musicals," she wondered outloud.

"Some, but I've been saving the good ones for you,"

I saw a few, including a weird magic show," she chuckled. "It was inspired by Penn & Teller….and I couldn't help but think of you all through the show."

"That's sweet," he nodded.

She then explained quite a few of the key events and experiences during her time in London. She didn't mention her time with Daniel, since it didn't result in anything naughty.

Marc had actually assumed that given her attractive looks and a whole semester abroad, she must have had a few dates. The fact is, he did too. After a few of his magic shows, some of the young women wanted to treat him to a beer afterwards. He graciously agreed, and actually went out with one of women a few times. It was fun, but led to nothing. Marc believed it was pointless to recount the non-details with Pat. Better to deal with the here and now…and perhaps even the promising future.

After dinner, Marc asked if Pat wanted to join him in his nearby apartment.

"Is your roommate out of town?" she asked.

"He's out of town at least half the time….and this is one of those out-of-town nights for him."

Pat smiled and reached across for Marc's hand. "I already told my parents I would probably be staying in town with a good friend," she said with a giggle.

"Am I that good friend?" he chucked back.

"Absolutely," she answered.

Not surprisingly, it was a fantastic, beautiful night for two people who truly missed each other, and longed to be in each other's embrace.

Chapter 29

A few weeks later, Marc invited Pat to a special evening in Manhattan.

He missed hearing her voice and had heard of a Karaoke Club where the participants could bring in an instrumental of their chosen song and sing in front a crowd of about 100 people.

He told Pat about it, and she agreed it could be great fun…. especially since she had not sung a song in front of people for about a year. In preparation, she practiced the song for several days, and remembered her long-ago voice teacher's advice to see someone/think of someone that she might be singing to.

That was easy, since he would be her date for the event. As a surprise, Pat had not told him the song.

"C'mon…give me a clue," he pleaded.

"No, I want to surprise you," she answered.

"Will I know it?" he asked.

"Yes, and you will love it." She just knew in her heart that the sentiment of the song would be right up his alley. When her name was called, she came to the stage and took the microphone like a pro. As the musical intro began to play, she spoke to the audience.

"I would like to dedicate this song to my friend, Marc….who early on—grade school I think—taught me the meaning of friendship. And then as we got older, as we are now—totally represents what it means to be in love. Marc, this is for you. That's What Friends are for.'"

With that, she began the lyric, "I never thought I'd feel this way…. Keep smiling. Keep shining. Knowing you can always count on me… That's what friends are for."

As the Dionne Warwick classic began to reach it's crescendo, Pat's voice soared….and a huge smile came across her face as she pointed to Marc.

When the song reached its finale, there was a least 30 seconds of applause and a standing ovation.

When she came to the table, Marc was still applauding and gave her a huge kiss on the lips. That just happened to generate more ovations from the appreciative audience.

After the courtesy of listening to a few other karaoke songs from the attendees, who admitted that was a very tough act to follow, Marc paid the bill and the couple strolled out of the Karaoke Club.

"That was the most amazing moment I have ever experienced," he told her with another kiss. "You, my dear Pat, are an fantastic talent, and must think about doing this seriously, and more frequently."

"It was thrilling for me to dedicate the song to you," she gushed and held him tighter.

"And it was thrilling for the audience," he told her. "And speaking of thrills, my roommate is out of town again."

"Wow, he's gone a lot," she remarked.

"Yeah, I think he's getting another job in a different city. And that's OK with me. I am probably making enough money at Tannen's to swing it by myself. Of course, it's always more fun to swing with you."

"I hope so," she giggled.

"Absolutely," he answered.

"By the way, on my way out of the Karaoke Club, the owner gave me the number of a couple of clubs where I could maybe get a gig with a live band."

"I think you should definitely try that," Marc replied. "You would get even more standing ovations. I'll go...and you don't even have to dedicate the song to me."

With that, she quietly reprised the musical phrase, "You've got a friend."

He completed the thought. "And since I do, I'll keep smiling. And keep shining."

They both did all night long with plenty of hugs and kisses and dreams about the future.

Chapter 30

In their final semesters at their respective colleges, both Marc and Pat fared well academically.

Marc had decided to major in business. Fortunately for him, he did not find the classes particularly difficult. Since there was no such thing as a major in magic (and he had enough work and shows to satisfy that passion), he thought perhaps a business degree might come in handy if he ever wanted to scale up his performances as a full-time business.

Pat's path was a little more complicated. Ever since she had been a high school student, her father had wanted her to major in journalism and follow in his footsteps. Ironically, she did like to write, but it didn't totally excite her as a full-time, post-college pursuit. In her younger days, she had seen how many late hours her dad had to put in just to meet publication deadlines. As luck would have it, in her first several years at NYU, she had taken many J-school classes here and in the London. She actually had quite a few credit hours already to ease into a journalism degree.

So what did excite her as a post-college livelihood? Bet you can guess: music! It had always made her heart beat a little quicker and the performance of songs truly did satisfy her. Her roles in musicals and her occasional gigs singing in clubs felt completely natural to her.... and as Marc had often told her, it's a rare, god-given talent that should never be wasted, Consequently, she rejiggered her classes and declared a double major.

It caused a little ruckus in the Foley household. Mr. Foley frankly thought it was folly to split her attention.

"I'll still get a journalism degree from NYU," she argued to her dad. "And I got good grades in all my writing classes.'

"That's because you're good at it," her dad replied.

"But I'm also good at music. Perhaps you've heard me sing?" she answered sarcastically. "Perhaps one day, I'll combine the two...but right now, I don't want to give up on my love of music."

There was a long pause. Finally, her mother chimed in and proved to be the voice of reason. "You know what, honey," she told her daughter. "It's a long life. And you're lucky you are good at more than one thing. Ultimately, you will need to follow your instincts and follow your heart."

There was another pause. Mrs. Foley looked at her husband and smiled at him. "You want your daughter to be happy, don't you," she said. "She will never lose your talent at writing. But we could all get hit by a meteor tomorrow. Meanwhile, we should enjoy every single day."

After a few seconds, Mr. Foley walked to Pat and put his arm around her shoulder. "Honey, I am in your corner. Always will be. No matter what corner you ultimately choose. I just hope I don't get hit by a meteor in that corner," he said with a laugh.

They all had a chuckle together and let the subject pass for now. *Time will tell*, Mr. Foley told himself.

When she told Marc the outcome of her discussion with her parents, he was tickled. As a further encouragement, he asked her when she might perform next.

"Funny, you should ask. You must be reading my mind. Just today, I called a few of the clubs that the manager of the Karaoke Club recommended." she proudly reported. "He had already called them and put in a good word for me."

"Do you know what you're going to sing?" Marc asked.

"Not yet. I've got a new voice teacher at NYU and I want to rehearse a few songs with her. The two clubs I contacted both said I would need to audition for them some afternoon. And I would need about three songs."

"That'll be a breeze for you," he assured her. "Can I come and give you moral support at your audition?"

"I think that would be very nice," Pat answered.

Pat's voice teacher at NYU, Carole Sherman, was a big fan of her young student. She loved Pat's renditions and personal interpretations.

Consequently, she took a great interest in the upcoming audition at the Flatiron Room.

To help, she suggested some songs that packed emotional wallop. She also recommended a talented pianist, Christina Walker, to accompany her. That way, they could practice together and perfect the timing.

After rehearsing several songs, they settled on three love songs: "What's New," which was made popular by Linda Ronstadt,

"Unchained Melody" from the Righteous Brothers, and "This Magic Moment," originally introduced by Jay and the Americans.

At the audition in early November, Michael Toomey, the manager of the Flatiron Room met all three of them in the lobby just prior to their scheduled 2:30 p.m. audition.

"Who is Pat the singer?" Michael asked and Pat raised her hand. "Pat, I am happy to meet you. The manager of Karaoke Club absolutely raves about you. In fact, he told me that you got the biggest applause in months."

"It was fun," Pat responded humbly.

And you, miss…" the manager turned to the other woman. "What is your name, and your role?"

"I am Christina Walker," she answered. "And I play the piano. I'm here to accompany my friend."

"That's great," Michael said. "Sounds like you both have rehearsed this a few times."

"And you, young man?" Michael turned to Marco. "Do you play the guitar?"

"Nahh, I'm a magician," Marc answered. "But I am mostly here for moral support, if that's alright."

"It's OK with me, if it's OK with you," the manager said to the two woman and both agreed. As the two men waited for the women to get on stage, they chatted.

"Do you perform magic on stage?" Michael asked.

"Sometimes. I've done Monday Night Magic in Manhattan."

"That's a big show," the manager shook his head affirmatively. He then turned to the two woman on stage, who had been miked up and were ready to present their songs. When they were ready, he introduced them as if it were a gig. "Ladies and Gentlemen, and now… the one-and-only Pat Foley, accompanied on the piano by her friend, Christine Walker. Let's give them a nice welcoming round of applause."

Instantly, Marc clapped his hands and the manager of the club did so as well to make them feel at ease.

Pat thanked them and nodded to her pianist to begin.

All three songs were then presented with panache and style.

As she finished the last of the three, "This Magic Moment," Michael, the manager of the club, gave a standing ovation. Pat graciously bowed, smiled and waved to the two men in the audience.

"That was absolutely fantastic!" Michael exclaimed. "How soon can you start?" Without waiting for an answer, the manager suggested three weekends in a row starting this weekend. He also promised to draw up a contract for tomorrow and have it for you to sign.

"Those dates are good for me," Pat responded. So did Christina.

He then looked at Marco. "I half-way expected you to get up and show some illusions on that last song—"This Magic Moment." If you're as good as they are, and the women are agreeable, maybe you could do that one night?"

"I'll leave it to them," Marco responded. "This is their moment in the sun."

"Good call," Michael nodded.

With that all three of them exited the club and screamed hooray on West 26th Street.

"I will have to call my mom and dad and make sure they are there for opening night."

"I'm sure they will be," Marc answered. "I will of course be there every night,"

"You better be," Pat giggled and gave him a big kiss for encouraging her every step of the way.

On December 15, Pat's family and fans got to the Flatiron Club by 6 p.m. to enjoy cocktails and dinner before her performance. Several of Pat's classmates from NYU attended, as well as Carol Sherman, her music professor. Mr. and Mrs. Foley along with Marc were seated near the front so they could enjoy her every note.

Pat and Christina did join them early on for a soft drink as they listened to a few jazz groups and solo singers. Mr. and Mrs. Foley seemed to be enjoying the ambiance of the club. Inside, it was a darkly lit place with a sophisticated audience.

Most of the groups were quite good, and Marc asked Pat if she was at all nervous.

"Not really," she answered and looked at her piano accompanist. "We're actually pretty well rehearsed." Indeed, they were. After a few hugs at the table, Pat motioned to her piano accompanist that it was probably time to wait backstage.

Around 7:30, Michael the manager took the stage and proudly introduced "one of the best singers I have heard in years,"—Miss Pat Foley, and her excellent accompanist, Christina Walker."

There was polite applause as they took the stage. With no further ado, Pat began singing her first number, "What's New?" As usual, there was something unusual in her voice and presentation that tended to quiet the audience and demand their attention. "Unchained Melody," also captured the attention of the room, but it was "This Magic Moment," that seemed to electrify the crowd. By the end of her finale, the crowd gave a thrilling ovation.

The two young women gratefully bowed and exited the stage. In a few minutes, they both rejoined the table. 'That was spectacular,"

Mr. and Mrs. Foley said. Mr. Foley even kidded Marco that perhaps he should get up and do some magic tricks when his daughter sang the last song.

"You're not the first person to suggest that," Marc responded, reflecting on the manager's similar suggestion. "But I wanted this to be her night in the spotlight." Mrs. Foley hugged her daughter as she took her seat. "Superb," Mr. Foley answered, and motioned that the waiter should bring two bottles of champagne, which he had preordered for the table. He poured glasses for the table and toasted his daughter. "I've got to admit, you really are a talent. I was enthralled, and I'm sure everyone at this table was as well."

Toasts for all. Lots of smiles. More music. After dessert, the crowd walked outside past the lobby, where the manager gave a big thumbs up to Pat.

After a sweet kiss on the sidewalk, Marc shook hands with Mr. and Mrs. Foley, and gave Pat a sweet kiss. In advance, she had told him that it would probably be best to spend the evening back in Westchester with her mom and dad. As he waved goodbye to his girlfriend, he was so proud of her spectacular accomplishment. Of course, he would miss her tonight, but he sincerely believed she had taken a big step on a brave new path.

Chapter 31

Over the next several months, Pat had several more gigs at The Flatiron Room. Just to keep things fresh and expand her horizons, she did vary her repertoire and her song selections.

In the meantime, Marco also broadened his routines with new performances on Monday Night Magic. One night, he would concentrate on mentalism. Another night, he would focus on flash and fire. Perhaps his favorite genre was to combine music with illusions. Not surprisingly, his favorite songs were the ones sung by Pat.

Ever since he had heard her sing "This Magic Moment" at the Flatiron Room, he wanted to combine illusions with her vocals. On the urging of Michael, the manager, he actually did create a joint appearance at the club one night to that song. It got the biggest applause of the evening, and encouraged him to pursue the combo of magic and music more regularly.

In so many ways, it was a perfect amalgamation. As he had often believed, music itself is a creative miracle, especially when presented by Pat. The lyrics always sounded surprising, spontaneous and extremely personal. Best of all, it gave both of them the opportunity to share their talents on the same stage.

Marco wanted to do showcase "This Magic Moment" at one of his Monday Night Magic shows. However, Pat had this odd feeling that it was a form of "double-dealing."

"Shouldn't we reserve that song for the Flatiron Room, where we first introduced it?" she asked. Reluctantly, Marc agreed.

"Don't worry," Pat promised him. "I'll come up with another great song that will meld with your great magic."

She researched a bunch of songs that had magic as a theme, but something compelled her to keep looking and listening. After several weeks, she decided to try a different route.

It would involve writing--a skill she had inherited from her father and learned from all those journalism classes. Despite her double-major these days, she continued to hone her writing skills.

In fact, she often wrote guest articles for her NYU college newspaper, called *The Washington Square News.* They were usually linked to show biz reviews of off-Broadways musicals, or club acts in town. Occasionally, she would venture into other territories. For example, she had written many opinion pieces: Best Christmas songs. Best musicals to see with your parents when they come to town. She had recently written an article about the best Valentine albums of all times.

As a source of pride, she would often find letters to the editor praising her work. Normally she would save the articles and send them to her father, who was proud of her achievements. "Hey, maybe you will actually find a career path that combines music and writing. Wouldn't that make you happy?"

Of course, it did. However, despite her many examples, she had never actually combined her writing with the creation of music. She had never written an original song, so far. But as Pat reflected on It, she smiled to herself and said "There's always a first time."

She tried several different approaches and many different titles, but eventually felt most comfortable with a version that captured the romance and discovery of magic. It was a love song in the style of Mariah Carey. The title: "Abracadabra. I love you."

If you listen to the radio, perhaps you're familiar with it. If not, here goes:

Abracadabra, I love you.

It's just the most amazing thing.
Somehow, it makes me want to sing
About the astonishing way I feel
Is it a miracle? Is it real?

Oh, It's a mind-blowing deal
And a phenomenal reveal
This emotion in my heart
I just knew it from the start.

Shazaam. Oh, this is good
Voila. I trust it's understood
How often and warmly I always think of you.
Abracabra. Oh, I love you.

No hocus pocus
No secret doors.
No tricky traps above you
Just abracadabra my dear heart
Abracadabra, I love you.

Abracadabra, my magical friend
Abracadabra, I love you.

Once she had the words on paper, she called her pianist friend, Christina, who turned the rhyme into a ballad with a beautiful bridge in the middle. After listening to a few times, both thought they had a winner. Consequently, they recorded a version, thanks to the music department of NYU.

Pat was excited to share the song with Marco. When she came to his apartment that evening, she brought a CD of the song.

With some fanfare, she asked Marc to sit down in a chair and prepare himself for a nice surprise.

"What is it?" he asked.

"It's an original song I created for your magic show. Just close your eyes and try to imagine the miracles you might perform to this music."

He did so. However, he couldn't help but react quickly to the emotion of the tune. Halfway through, he started to cry. By the end of the song, he was completely in tears.

After it sunk in, he slowly rose from his chair, and gave Pat the biggest kiss of his life. "Abracabara, I love you too," he sobbed. "That's the most heart-stopping gift I have ever received," he added. "I can't believe my ears."

He started writing down possible tricks that might go with the lyric, but soon decided to put the paper aside. He could do that later. For now, he wanted to share the greatest sex of his life with the woman of his dreams.

It was a night they would never forget.

Chapter 32

wo months later, he debuted the new routine at Monday Night Magic.

He had invited Michael, the manager at Tannen's. his mom and dad, and his Uncle Ray, who had seen many of his shows. Like Mr. and Mrs. Obie, Ray was extremely proud of Marc's accomplishments, and had followed his blossoming career throughout the years.

Pat had had also invited her mother and father, her collaborator Christina, and many friends from the staff of *the New Amsterdam News.*

In anticipation of the event, Marc held the outstretched hand of Pat and winked at her. "This is going to be great…" he said enthusiastically, "…thanks to you."

"Hope so," she smiled back.

When the emcee announced his name, Marc walked to the stage holding hands with Pat.

When the applause tapered off, he started speaking, "Ladies and Gentlemen, welcome to Monday Night Magic…and music! I say music, too…because my dear girlfriend, Pat Foley, who has sung in many clubs here in Manhattan, wrote an original song just for this performance. "

"I hope you enjoy the magic, and I hope you enjoy the music as much as I do. Pat, shall we begin?"

As he asked the question, she hit the button on her tape recorder machine and began to hum to the lead-in instrumental. As she did so, Marc unveiled a large bright red scarf and showed both sides.

As he did so, Pat began to sing:

"It's just the most amazing thing.

Somehow, it makes me want to sing.."

Over the lyric *"Is it a miracle? Is it real?"* Marc shook the large silk and revealed a large human-sized microphone, which he rolled over to Pat.

He then showed a large bag and showed the empty contents to the audience. He immediately reached in the air, and made a card appear out of his right hand. Then another. Then another.

As Pat sang, "Oh it's a mind-blowing deal and phenomenal reveal, Marco dumped an entire deck of cards into the bag. He then showed the contents of the bag to again be empty. With some panache, he then seemed to reach into the bag, and pulled out a large red inflated heart. Over the lyric, "the emotion in my heart…." He carried it by the attached string, and presented it to Pat.

"Shazaam. Oh, this is good.

Voila. I trust it's understood….

As Marc heard her lyric, he reached his left hand in the air, and when he opened his hand, white grains of salt poured into his right hand. When he opened that hand, two butterflies flew out of his palm into the audience.

"No hocus pocus.

No secret doors…"

The magician reached in his lapel and took out a flower. He then reached into his jacket, took out another silk and covered that flower with the silk. He then reached in his other pocket and pulled out a magic wand. After hitting the silk twice, he pulled the silk away and revealed a vase full of roses.

"Abracadabra, my dear heart.

Abracadabra, I love you."

As Pat repeated the phrase, he presented the roses to her, and the two of the them took a bow to thunderous applause. In fact, it was a standing ovation.

After several bows, the two of them blew the audience a kiss and returned to their table.

Once the crowd began to eventually quiet down, Uncle Ray ordered champagne for the entire table and poured glasses for all.

"I think that is one of the best performances I have ever seen," he toasted them.

"I agree," Mr. Foley said. "Wow, you two are damn good together."

Pat and Marco toasted thanked him for the compliment and basked in the afterglow. Out of courtesy, they watched the entire show of four other performers. All in all, a bravissimo night for everyone.

Chapter 33

In the ensuing months before their graduations, Marc and Pat tried to spend as much time together as possible. It felt natural for both of them.

However, the still had classes to attend, and work requirements. As Marc got closer to his business degree, Otto, the manager of Tannen's, couldn't help but notice that his favorite young magician also had a good head for inventory, sales, and publicity. Consequently, he had spoken to Marco about perhaps becoming the assistant manager of the store and increasing his weekly shows. In addition to his commitment to the Tannen's, Marc also performed regularly on Monday Night Magic.

Pat had her plate full as well. Given her prowess with the written word, she was named assistant editor of the NYU newspaper. Just to keep things in balance, she also had a few singing performances at various Manhattan Clubs.

Every once in a while, they would perform together, which was their biggest thrill. As a matter of fact, they considered auditioning as a duo on *America's Got Talent*. However, that would have to wait. With their busy schedules and upcoming graduations, they wanted to value every minute together.

Often, they would just shoot the breeze with each other, and escape the hubbub of Manhattan. On other nights, they would lose themselves in a late night movie. Sometimes, they would cook a quick meal together and have a few laughs about the absurdity of the day-to-day. Inevitably, they would sometimes dream of days to come.

They both sincerely believed that they would inevitably live under the same roof and perhaps explore their passions together. Having known each other for more than a dozens years (and having experienced some other relationships), they each wondered about the "m" word. Rather than confront it, each one simply teased the other about "how perfect" they were together.

One late night, that code-language became more explicit.

"Do you think we will be together two years from now?" he asked.

"I do," she answered.

"Five years from now?"

"I do."

"Ten years from now?"

"I do." She again answered.

"I like the sound of that." Marc said.

"You do?"

"I do."

After a good 15 seconds, Marc swallowed hard and popped the question. "I would like to marry you," he proposed.

After a slightly longer pause, Pat snuggled next to him and looked him in the eyes. "You do?" she asked, and then she answered her own question.

"I do."

Instinctively, the two of them engaged in a passionate kiss. They were both all smiles, and filled with spontaneous energy. Marco held her hand and motioned for them to go to the kitchen table.

"How do we go about this?" he asked.

"I would say we wait till we graduate before we tell anyone. Maybe at our graduation parties, we tell our parents…and then we plan for a big celebration at the end of summer or early fall."

"Wow, you think we can keep it a secret until then?" he wondered outloud.

"I hope so," she replied. "Otherwise, it will occupy our every minute just answering questions—who, what, where, when, etc. etc. etc. Besides, wouldn't it be fun to just bask in our private bliss for a while?"

As he thought about, he smiled broadly. Then he took her hand and walked back to the bed together. Gently, they both hugged and gently caressed each other. It was perhaps the most heavenly evening either one had ever spent.

The months seemed to fly by at super speed. As luck would have it, both Pat and Marco graduated in early June with just a week between both commencement events. Each attended the other's ceremony, along with the the graduate's parents. Afterwards, there was a celebratory lunch at fancy Manhattan restaurant. It was all Marco could do to not blurt out the big news beginning with "m." Same thing with Pat. However both agreed to keep the graduation ceremonies pure and focused. Afterwards, each agreed to break the news to their respective parents before their graduation parties. At that time, both agreed that it would be ideal to announce it to close friends and relatives.

At Pat's celebration, her father spoke first to the crowd. He used the opportunity to thank everyone for attending and brag about his dear daughter. "Ever since she was a kid, she was a model student…. and that continued all through college. For those who don't know, she graduated with two majors: journalism, which always puts a smile on face. And music, which always makes my heart soar.

"I wish her all the best in the days ahead, and speaking of that---I would like to have Pat come up here, and spread some news about the days ahead. "

She joined her dad, gave him a hug and thanked him for everything. She then addressed the crowd. "So I always wondered, what do you do after college? Get a real job? Get a masters? Travel all over? Chase your dreams?

"Let me deal with the last one: Chase your dreams. And I have found a way to do that—not all by myself, but with a kindred spirit who brings me great happiness, encouragement, and yes—love. His name is Marc Obie. Raise your hand Marc! Many of you know him. But what you don't know is that in the next several months, we will marry. And I couldn't be happier.

"So t his is a double-whammy! A graduation party and an engagement announcement. I hope many of you can make the wedding. But for now, let's enjoy all that this afternoon can bring, and all that tomorrow promises."

There was a hearty applause, and a wonderful celebration. Pat introduced Marc to people who didn't know him, and also spent plenty of time with her parents and grandparents, who were truly happy for her.

It wss déjà vu one week later in the Obie backyard. Well, OK— given their middle-class roots, it was slightly different. Instead of a buffet spread, it was a barbecue. The graduation gifts were undoubtedly more humble. However, the good cheer was every bit as festive.

As the evening came to a close, Marc asked for everyone's attention so he could raise a toast to all attendees. "First of all, I want to thank my mom and dad who raised me with the right values. I want to thank my Uncle Ray who taught me magic as a young boy. But I also want to thank someone who is standing over here in front. Her name is Pat Foley. Wave to the people, Pat! She was my first true friend at Hastings Grade School. She's the first person I ever performed a trick for—and she kept it a secret. Never told anyone how it was done! How about that, Uncle Ray? She encouraged me to go to college. And she's the best damn singer in whole wide world. Oh, and one other thing… she's going to be my wife!"

There was a slight head-jolt for many of the people in the audience, which was followed by quick applause.

"I want to thank all of you for coming this afternoon, and I hope you can all come to our wedding—probably in late summer or early fall."

There was another big round of applause, followed by introductions and toasts in the evening.

Chapter 34

Marc and Pat had looked forward to this day for many months. In private, each had dreamed of the big day for years.

September 5 turned out to be a picturesque afternoon for a wedding. Warm, but not hot. Just a few clouds in the sky. A very slight breeze to add a little pep in everyone's step.

Sacred Heart Church in Dobbs Ferry was the favored venue for the bride and groom. It was an historical church with stained glass windows and a beautiful fancy alter with lots of glitter. Of all the churches in the area, it was the one they both attended on big days like Christmas and Easter. And on this --biggest day of their lives-- it was exactly perfect.

Both of Pat's voice teachers through the years were bridesmaids. Christine, her piano accompanist was also in the wedding party, as was her college roommate from her early years at NYU.

Marco's wedding party included his boss from Tannen's, a few of his local friends, and his Uncle Ray, who served as his best man.

The Church was packed with people, with a reserved front pew for Marc's and Pat's parents. Not surprisingly, her grandparents had flown in from Europe just to witness this lovely event, and also had a front row seat.

As the organist started to play Arioso by J.S. Bach, the procession began when the groomsman and bridesmaids began to walk towards the alter. Eventually, the focus of the church was on Marco, who was all smiles to all the guests and his wedding party, and happily awaited his dear bride.

After a slight pause, Mr. Foley walked his beautiful daughter down the center aisle, and then gave her a big hug and a kiss when they reached the front. He also shook Marco's hand, and then joined his wife in the front reserved pew.

During the service, the priest, Father Zipfel (who knew both the bride and groom from their attendance at Sacred Heart). spoke about the importance of shared interests and referenced how proud he was that both Marc and Pat were pursuing creative paths together. He even avowed that such pursuits were "a lovely embodiment of God's grace and an inspiration for all our fellow human beings."

When he asked the couple to exchange their vows, Marc could barely contain himself since he was so thrilled to marry the woman of his dreams.

"Marc, repeat after me," the priest said. "I, Marc take you Pat to be my wife. I promise to be good to you in good times and bad."

When it was Pat's turn, she gladly complied, and continued, "…in sickness and in health, I will love you and honor you all the days of my life."

Pat was particularly tickled, especially when the priest announced that the couple could exchange rings. They looked beautiful and fit perfectly.

The couple was beaming, and when the pastor announced that Marc could kiss the bride, he did a loving embrace and sweet kiss, in keeping with the church ceremony.

True to the mood, the organist played Amazing Grace during communion.

After a few closing thoughts, the processional at the end was Ode to Joy by Beethoven, which exactly summed up the emotion of the moment.

As impressive as the wedding ceremony was, the reception was an event that would undoubtedly be remembered by all. For starters, it was held at the Lyndhurst Mansion in nearby Tarrytown, New York.

This place was originally zillionaire Jay Gould's estate. Today, the Gothic Revival Country estate sits majestically on a 67-acre site overlooking the Hudson River. Thanks to his business connections, Mr. Foley was able to negotiate this once-in-lifetime experience for a wedding reception.

It was an elegant, museum-like venue with gourmet cuisine and a full orchestra, which Pat had pre-arranged from the Flatiron Club.

Everyone danced. Everyone dined. Everyone looked beautiful in their dressed-up fancy attire.

How could the evening possibly be better?

Wait… perhaps one more thing: original music.

For their first wedding dance, Pat and Marc had rehearsed the

group to play their favorite tune. For many of the out-of-towners in the room, it was the first time they had heard it.

If you listen to the radio in the U.S, you probably know the rendition popularized by that certain new singing sensation called Pat Foley.

The closing refrain goes like this:

Abracadabra, I love you.
Abracadabra, Yes, my dear.
I'm so happy when you're near.
Abracadabra, Oh, yes. Oh, yes.
    Oh, yes. Oh, yes.
Abracadabra, I love you.

www.ingramcontent.com/pod-product-compliance
Lightning Source LLC
Chambersburg PA
CBHW050004070726
47592CB00018B/800